"Just who do you think you are?"

Stacy's voice was shrill. "Humiliating me like that in front of your cowboys! Well, I'll show you, Mr. Big Shot. I can take anything you can dish out!"

"Oh, can you?" Cord murmured savagely. His mouth descended on Stacy's in a kiss meant to hurt, to punish, to master her completely. Then he pushed her away.

Stacy was stunned by her passionate response to him. "All right, you've proved your point," she said finally. "You know you can always force me to 'behave.'" Her eyes darkened with emotion. "But you will never, ever be able to make me feel anything but disgust for you!"

JANET DAILEY

No Quarter Asked

Harlequin Books

TORONTO • NEW YORK • LONDON
AMSTERDAM • PARIS • SYDNEY • HAMBURG
STOCKHOLM • ATHENS • TOKYO • MILAN

The original edition published April 1990
Second printing August 1990

ISBN 373-83213-3

Harlequin Presents edition published January 1976
Janet Dailey Treasury edition 1985

Original hardcover edition published in 1974
by Mills & Boon Limited

CHAPTER ONE

STACY STARED out the window at the traffic rushing between the concrete buildings below. The sombre grey and brown tones of the towering structures reflected the depression that hung so heavy on the young girl's shoulders. A little sigh escaped her as she let the curtain fall back in place and turned to face the ageing man behind the desk.

"Mr. Mills, you were Daddy's friend. You should understand more than anyone why I have to get away by myself to sort things out. Why does it have to make any difference if it's in a New York apartment or a cabin in Texas?"

"It's because I was your father's attorney and closest friend that I wish you would think it over a little more," the lawyer replied, removing his black-rimmed glasses and absently wiping them with his handkerchief.

"I'm not trying to run away," Stacy ran a gloved hand nervously over her arm. "I just need time to see where I fit in again."

"Look, Stacy, any other young girl in your shoes would be going to Europe or the Islands. You're a wealthy girl now. I can understand that you aren't particularly happy with the way you acquired your money, but the death of someone dear always involves a difficult adjustment. You've always been so independent, even headstrong, that I don't see why you insist on burying yourself out in the country.''

Stacy Adams looked hesitantly at Carter Mills, Sr., wondering how she could make him understand why she had to go. Her father, Joshua Adams, had respected this man and trusted him as few men are ever able to in their lifetime. *Her father*. The words caught in her throat. Stacy glanced down at her blue suit and the gloved hands clenched so tightly in her lap. Her mother had died shortly after Stacy was born, leaving her globe-trotting husband with the unfamiliar and frightening task of raising their child. Refusing the generous offers from friends to care for Stacy, Joshua Adams had filled another suitcase with nappies and powder and carted the year-old girl off on his next foreign assignment. Life for father and daughter had been one long world tour with brief respites in New York to catch their breath before starting out again, as he built his reputation as a freelance photographer.

Loving memories whirled through Stacy's mind, most vividly, her seventeenth birthday three years ago, when her dad had smuggled a puppy into a plush New Orleans hotel. Cajun, he had called the pup, in honour of the Creole country of his birth. The wiggling, playful dog had swiftly grown into a husky German Shepherd, devoted entirely to his young mistress. Her father predicted that Cajun would protect Stacy better than any guardian angel. Stacy wondered if her father knew how right he had been, because it was Cajun who had pulled an unconscious but unharmed

Stacy from the wreckage of the chartered plane before it burst into flames. The pilot and her father didn't make it.

As she tried to blink back the tears that clouded her eyes, Stacy raised her head to meet the lawyer's affectionate gaze. Her brown eyes grew misty with the threatening tears, as her mouth curved into a painful smile.

"I take it back, Stacy. Perhaps going out there will help you face your problems. Joshua loved the West and never turned down an assignment that would take him there." Carter Mills, Sr., rose from his chair and walked around to where Stacy was seated. "But remember you're still a young woman, barely twenty, with a lot of the world ahead of you. He wouldn't have wanted you to miss any of it—not the good and definitely not the bad."

Stacy grasped the hands he offered and rose, her trim, tailored suit enhancing the feminine figure underneath. "I knew you would understand and see why I have to do this."

"There's at least one young man that I know of who's rather upset about your leaving," Carter Mills commented. "But you can't blame my son for wanting to escort you around our more fashionable clubs. And you can't say you don't belong there, not with the inheritance your father left you."

"I'm afraid I haven't accepted the idea that I'm comfortably wealthy yet. Before I was happy just to be with Dad, travelling wherever the wind blew—maybe I inherited his itchy feet. Out there with just Cajun, Diablo, and miles of space, I should be able to decide about the future,'' Stacy concluded as she reached for her purse.

"Are you taking that fool horse, too? I had hoped you'd sold him long ago," exclaimed the lawyer with no attempt to hide his concern. "I don't mind telling you that I think you're making a grave mistake taking him."

"Oh, Diablo isn't as vicious and unruly as you would like to believe. He's high-strung, that's all!" Stacy smiled. "You know very well that I'm an excellent horsewoman. Dad would never have allowed me to have Diablo if he didn't think I could handle him."

"I realize that, but I'm sure it never occurred to him that you would be taking that horse out in the wilds with you," Mr. Mills replied gruffly.

"No. I'm sure Dad probably hoped that I would settle down and take my place in society, so to speak. But I'm not ready for that yet. Maybe I never will want to be, who knows?" she said, then added, "I really should be going."

"What are you doing with the apartment while you're gone?"

"I decided to just lock it up rather than let it go," answered Stacy, a shadow of pain clouding her eyes momentarily.

"Just as long as you know you're always welcome at our home. And if there's ever anything you need, don't hesitate one minute," Carter Mills said.

"I won't. Carter Jr. is taking me to dinner tomorrow night for one last fling with civilization. He seems to think that I'm going to the darkest regions of Africa." Stacy smiled, touched by the sincere concern extended by the lawyer. "Thanks for everything, Mr. Mills."

Stacy smiled as she walked out of his office into the reception room. Mr. Mills couldn't help but have misgivings about her impending trip. She wasn't going to an exactly remote area, but she would be reasonably isolated. When his son Carter had told him about Stacy's decision to rent a hunting cabin in the Apache Mountains of Texas for the spring, he had immediately checked into the situation as a personal friend. But he honestly could find no real flaws with her plans, except that she was going alone.

Stacy entered the lift with a lighted "down" arrow flickering above it. Mulling over her plans, she was unaware of the interested looks she received from some of her fellow passengers. The sprinkling of freckles across a too-straight nose usually dismissed her, in a stranger's eye, as average. But second glances noticed the gleaming brown hair framing her oval face and the dark brown eyes, now shadowed by her grief, with their naturally thick lashes that combined to give her a refreshingly wholesome aura.

On the ground floor, Stacy proceeded to the street where an incessant tide of pedestrians awaited the commands of the red and green globes. Swept along by the flow at the crosswalk, she let herself be led by the steady stream until she reached the parking lot where she had left her car. Preoccupied with her memories as she was, her hand caressed the steering wheel for a second before accelerating into the traffic. The luxurious sports car had been the last present her father had given her.

Looking back, Stacy realized she should have recognized the import the expensive gift carried. She had always assumed that, although she and her father lived very comfortably, their financial condition was dependent on her father's income. The discovery that her father's death had left her independently wealthy still seemed a dream. Stacy didn't know what she would have done if that had not been the case. She possessed a smattering of knowledge about everything, but she had forgone any further schooling to travel with her father.

Arriving at her apartment building, Stacy entered and took the lift to the fifth floor. Silently she walked down the corridor to her apartment and hesitated as she reached her door. Depression spread over her as she inserted the key and opened the door. She was immediately greeted by an ecstatic German Shepherd yelping his pleasure at her return.

"Cajun, you brute, did you miss me?" Stacy smiled sadly, cradling the enormous head in her hands as she looked at the unmasked adoration in the dog's eyes. "What would I do if you weren't here?"

The telephone jingled dimly, stirring Stacy out of her thoughts. Bending a nyloned knee on the flowered couch, she picked up the receiver.

"Yes?"

"Stacy? Carter," came the masculine voice on the other end. "Dad said I just missed you."

"I left there around four," Stacy said, glancing at her watch as she sat on the couch.

"How's everything going?" A touch of concern peeped out of the light tone.

"Fine, really. I was just going to finish up the last of my packing, except for the few odds and ends that will have to wait," Stacy said, adding with a little laugh, "I even packed some dresses in with all my riding clothes. I'm planning to live it up in some little cowtown!"

"Just as long as you don't meet some tall, dark, handsome cowboy and ride off into the sunset on his trusty steed," Carter mocked, "I won't mind."

"I wouldn't worry. They don't make cowboys like they used to," Stacy chuckled. "On our last trip west, all I ever saw were sunburned, middle-aged men with families to support."

"Are you still driving down?"

"Just Caj and me. Diablo's going by train as far as Pecos. I'll pick him up there and go on to McCloud. The cabin's about thirty miles from town, so I'm really not too far from civilization."

"I'm glad you didn't ask me to go along. All that solitude would drive me up the wall. I don't see how you'll be able to take it for more than a week. How different can one mountain be from another?" Carter teased.

"Maybe you're right, but I'll have to find that out for myself."

"Can't talk you out of a thing, can I?" the voice in the receiver said. "Listen, I have a brief to work on tonight, so I won't be able to come round. We still have a date for tomorrow night. Seven sharp, right?"

"Right," Stacy agreed.

"Okay. Take care and I'll see you tomorrow. 'Bye!"

"Good-bye, Carter."

The click of the phone echoed forlornly in the crushing silence that followed. Refusing to give in to the melancholy that the empty room emitted, Stacy rose from the flowered couch to enter her bedroom. She would do that last-minute packing she had mentioned, filling the void intensified by the phone call with a bustle of activity.

THE NEXT night Stacy was just fastening the clasp on her onyx pendant when the doorbell rang. She surveyed her reflection one last time in the mirror. The sleeveless, peach-coloured dress with its V-neck and pleated skirt set off the copper tan of her skin and the golden highlights in her hair, that was pulled back in ringlets, Grecian style. Taking a tissue, Stacy blotted her peach-tinted lips and applied a little gloss before allowing a satisfied smile to light her face.

When she opened the door to admit Carter, her dark eyes were flashing with pleasure. "I didn't keep you waiting too long, did I?"

The tall, fair-haired man grasped her hands and pushed her away from him. His blue eyes answered her sparkle with a shine all their own. "May I say what you already know? I wouldn't have minded waiting longer if I'd known what a vision I was going to see. Shall we go?" he asked, placing the crocheted stole Stacy handed him around her shoulders while brushing a light kiss on her hair. "I've made reservations for eight at the Meadow Wood Country club."

"Marvellous," Stacy smiled.

The two chatted amiably on their way to his car, but once inside the conversation abated. Carter gave his full attention to the traffic around him while Stacy unobtrusively studied his silhouette. He was a good-looking man with light brown, almost blond hair and clear blue eyes. Six years older than Stacy and just entering his father's law practice, Carter was considered quite a catch by many of her acquaintances. His attractive fair looks were a perfect foil for Stacy's brown hair and eyes.

There had never been any avowals of love or promises to wait between them. When Stacy had accompanied her father on his travels, she had sent Carter funny postcards of wherever she was and called him when she got back in town. Carter dated other girls when she was gone, but never anyone as regularly as Stacy. The two families had been pleased with the budding relationship of their children, nurturing secret hopes of an eventual marriage.

Stacy smiled, watching the competent hands manoeuvring the car into a parking lot. Their relationship could never be considered as brother-and-sister, she thought, even if it hadn't reached the heart-pounding passionate stage yet. They were both enjoying the other's company while waiting for love to come their way. Some day, she supposed, they would marry. They would have a good life. They got along together too well for it to be any other way. But not yet, not yet.

"Besides," Stacy thought, "I'm still naïve enough to wish for a love that will sweep me off my feet, even if it is only fairy-tale stuff."

"Dreamer, are you going to get out of the car or just sit there?" Carter asked, laughing down at the girl as he stood holding the car door open for her.

"I'm sorry—I was off in another world."

"Well, come back. Tonight is my night and I plan to make the most of it," he smiled as he escorted her to the club entrance.

His arm rested lightly around her waist as he opened the elaborately scrolled doors of the private club. Carter ordered their drinks while Stacy gazed at the unique furnishings. The bar was decorated in an exotic jungle-type atmosphere with leopard and zebra skins adorning the walls.

When the waitress returned with their drinks, Stacy caught Carter looking at her with a sombre expression on his face.

"Why so grim? I thought we were going to celebrate tonight?" Stacy chided.

"Sorry, I was thinking about that vacation you're taking. Stacy, Dad isn't too happy about it, and neither am I. If anything happened to you out at that godforsaken cabin, it could be weeks before anyone finds out," he said earnestly.

"Please, let's don't talk about it tonight. I've made up my mind that I'm going and that's all there is to be said," she replied a little sharply because of her own apprehension. "It seems everyone knows what's best for me but me."

"Did it ever occur to you that this time they might be right?" A hint of disgust was in his voice. "You seem to think that because you've travelled all over the world you can handle anything that may happen. Why, you're no more experienced than some country girl! All your father showed you was the world from the sheltered side of a camera lens. You have no idea what it's like to be on your own."

"Just because I've seen war and hunger and famine from his view, does that make it any less real? I know what life is about. And I know what I'm going to do with mine, so there's no need of discussing it any further," Stacy retorted.

"Will you stop being so stubborn for once and listen to reason?"

"I told you the subject is closed."

"Then let's dance," Carter suggested roughly as the combo started playing a slow tune.

Stacy rose, pushing her chair back from the table. Carter held her elbow firmly, directing her to the dance floor. When he took her in his arms, both expressions were a little grim.

Stacy laughed, "Oh, Carter, I'm sorry. I really didn't mean to lose my temper. Please don't let's argue tonight."

He smiled down at the girl's pleading eyes. "Okay, we'll consider the subject closed. We'll just enjoy our evening together."

Later when their reservation for dinner was called, the couple entered the dining room and were escorted to a small table for two secluded from the rest of the diners. When the final course was over, the couple settled back contentedly with their coffee.

"That was a delicious meal," Stacy said, accepting the light from Carter for her cigarette.

"Umm. But the partner is even more delicious."

"Thank you, kind sir."

"Did you want to go back into the bar and dance, or would you rather go somewhere else?"

"No, let's stay here. I really enjoy this atmosphere and besides, I don't feel in the mood for a discotheque tonight," Stacy replied.

"Good, neither do I. There's some talking I want to do and I'd hate to shout it over the din of some rock band."

"Please, not another lecture about my trip," she begged. "You promised there'd be no more discussion about my going to Texas."

"And I have every intention of keeping my word. This is something entirely different. Shall we go?"

"Yes."

Stacy waited for Carter at the entry way to the lounge while he paid the bill. They found a table over in a corner and ordered drinks. At the beginning of a slow ballad, they wound their way on to the floor. Holding Stacy a little away from him, Carter gazed down into her brown eyes and smiled gently.

"Remember after your father's funeral the comment Dad made about you being one of the family?"

"Yes," said Stacy, returning the serious look on her partner's face.

"I want to make it legal. I want you to be my wife," he said, their steps almost ceasing. "I'm not trying to talk you out of your trip, but while you're thinking about the future, I want you to include me. Stacy, I care about you—I love you and I want to watch over you for the rest of my life. We've never talked about the future before and it's time we did. Before, we were both too young. I still had law school to finish and you still had some growing up to do. Well, they're both done now and this is the time to start planning the rest of our lives."

"Carter, I don't know what to say. I don't know if I'm ready to settle down. I don't know—"

"Don't say anything. I know it's awfully soon after losing your father. You're bound to be confused, so I'm not asking for an answer yet. When I think you're ready, I'll ask you again properly. Until then I'm just asking you to remember that I love you and want to marry you while you're out there in that Texas refuge," Carter said quietly, gently kissing the top of her forehead.

He drew her once again into the circle of his arms, and they continued their dancing in silence while Stacy mulled the proposal over in her mind. She shouldn't have been surprised by it, but she was despite her earlier thoughts on the same line. Returning to their table after the song was over, they sat quietly without speaking.

"You mentioned you were shipping Diablo to Texas. I was going to ask if you wanted to take my grey," said Carter. "He's definitely more manageable than that red devil of yours."

"I don't expect to have much trouble with Diablo, but thanks for offering," Stacy said, smiling at her date. "Besides, he's already on his way to Pecos, so I'll just stick with my original arrangement."

"What time do you plan to leave tomorrow?" Carter asked.

"I hope to get started by midday."

"It's rather late now. I don't want it to be said that I kept you from your beauty rest. I think you'll have plenty to think about tonight. At least I hope so," said Carter, casually referring to his earlier proposal.

They talked little on the way home. Stacy nestled down in her seat and gazed out the window at the neon world before her. Pulling into the parking lot of Stacy's apartment building, Carter turned the car motor off, then instead of getting out of the car, he sat quietly in his seat looking at the brown-haired girl beside him.

"I won't be able to come over tomorrow and tell you good-bye, so I'll wish you my good luck now," he said, drawing her over into his arms.

Stacy tilted her head back and awaited his kiss. His lips were firm and gentle as they pressed down upon hers. He held her body close to his as his hands caressed the tanned shoulders underneath her stole. Stacy's heart increased its tempo with the growing urgency in his kiss.

"Take that with you, Stacy, and let it plead my cause," he finished.

Reluctantly Stacy stepped out of the car when he came around and opened the door for her. In silence, they walked into the building to the elevator.

"I'll leave you here. Stacy, come home soon," Carter whispered to her, looking down affectionately at the freckled nose and wide brown eyes. Softly he dropped a kiss on her forehead and walked away.

Watching the slender, but muscular man leave, Stacy felt a cold emptiness chill her heart. She turned uncertainly to the yawning doors of the lift. Quietly she let herself into the apartment, questioning her decision to leave the only home and friends she had.

An hour later she had fallen asleep, once again resolved to carry through with her plans to journey to Texas.

CHAPTER TWO

"McCloud—10 Miles," the sign read. Stacy arched her back, stretching the cramped muscles. Two and a half days of steady driving were beginning to tell. But she was almost there and the excitement of finally reaching her destination was starting to flow through her. She glanced briefly at her reflection in the rear view mirror. Only her eyes showed the weariness she felt from the long drive. The pale, lemon-yellow top that complemented her olive-green pant-suit looked as fresh as when she had put it on that morning. The matching jacket lay over the back of the passenger seat where Cajun was sleeping, his huge body contorted by the limited space.

The two-horse trailer specially designed for the Jaguar was pulling easily. Diablo had raised quite a fuss when she loaded him in Pecos, but had since settled down nicely.

The afternoon sun was glaring through the windshield of her car as Stacy reached for the sunglasses lying on the dash. It wouldn't be long now before she'd be in her Texas retreat. First she would stop in town to look up the Nolans, so they could direct her to the cabin and then pick up some groceries. With luck she should be cooking her supper by seven.

Ahead she could see the growing outline of the small town. As it drew closer, Stacy lowered her speed, taking in as much of the surroundings as she could.

She pulled into a petrol station on the outskirts of town. Stepping out of the black sports car, she snapped her fingers to the waking Shepherd to follow. Stiffly and a little sleepily, he joined his mistress on the concrete paving. Stacy glanced appreciatively around the station, noting the lack of litter and usual car parts. Although the building wasn't modern, it was in excellent repair.

A teenage boy walked out of the office area towards the Jaguar. His admiring glance at the lithe figure passed unnoticed by Stacy as she surveyed the town ahead of her, shimmering in the afternoon sun.

"Fill 'er up, miss?" the young voice drawled.

"Please. Check under the hood, too," she replied, smiling at the gentle Southern accent.

Cajun went off to investigate a grassy lot next to the station while Stacy walked into the office to escape the sun. Inside, it took a minute for her eyes to adjust to the absence of the blinding sunlight. There were two men inside. One, the older of the two, was dressed in an attendant's uniform. The other, who had his back to Stacy, was dressed in blue Levi's and a faded plaid shirt. His dark, almost black hair was barely visible under the sweat-stained brown Stetson on his head. His tall, muscular frame blocked the attendant's view of Stacy until she stepped over to the counter where there was a selection of sweets.

"S'cuse me, Cord. Can I help you, miss?" the man inquired.

Stacy glanced up at the man facing her, taking in the smiling hazel eyes and his creased face, leathered by the Texas sun. She couldn't help but return the smile offered by the stocky man.

"Yes, I'd like one of those chocolate bars," Stacy said.

"Sure thing," the man nodded, turning towards the cash register with the coins Stacy had handed him for the bar. "Don't think me nosey, ma'am, but from your accent, I take it you're not from around here?"

Laughing, Stacy replied, "I never realized I had an accent, but I suppose to you I do. Actually I'm from New York, but I'm staying here this summer. I was wondering if you could tell me where I might find a family named Nolan. I've rented their hunting cabin," she explained.

It was then that the second man turned to face Stacy, and she was surprised by the seeming antagonism in his eyes. Puzzled, she heard him mutter a good-bye to the man behind the counter and stride out the door to a jeep parked beside the station. Turning back to the counter, she attempted to shake herself free of that haunting expression in his eyes. What had she done?

"I'm sorry, what did you say?" she asked, realizing the attendant had been addressing her.

"I said the Nolans run the grocery store in town. You turn right at the next block, then straight for two more, then left. Theirs is the second shop from the corner," he smiled.

"Thank you."

"Miss, you were a quart low on oil, so I put some in. Boy, that's some car you got," the young boy commented, coming inside, his allegiance switching from the attractive girl to the black sports car. "I'll bet she really leaves 'em behind on the straight-away!"

"That's enough, Billy," the older man put in, taking Stacy's money for the petrol and oil. "I'm sure the lady appreciates the fact you like her choice of cars."

Stacy laughed in return. "Right now I'd better look up the Nolans or it'll be dark before I get to my new home."

"Well, you just follow the directions I gave you and you can't miss it. Molly Nolan is always there in the afternoons, and I imagine she'll know where to run down her old man," the attendant said as he walked along with Stacy to her car.

She whistled to Cajun and waved a good-bye to the two attendants as she drove out on to the highway. Stacy smiled to herself as she turned right at the next block. The people seemed friendly anyway. At least two of them were, she qualified. And she wasn't going to let a dark-haired stranger's seeming hostility spoil her first visit to the town. If he hadn't seemed so disagreeable, she probably would have considered him handsome, she reflected.

He certainly had the requirements—dark hair, brown eyes, and a tall, muscular build—but he had acted as if she carried the plague. There really wasn't any reason for her to keep dwelling on those unfriendly dark eyes; chances were she probably would never see him again. It was the clear-cut features of his face with their straight lines outlining his jaw, cheekbones, and chin that gave Stacy the feeling there was no "give" in the man.

Reaching the corner of the second block, she spied the grocery store. Ahead of her was a space just wide enough for her to park her car and trailer. Cajun attempted to join her when she hopped out of the car, but she ordered him to stay. She glanced into the horse van at Diablo before continuing on her way to the shop.

It was a quaint little main street, covering all of two or three blocks. There was a drugstore on the corner, the grocery store next to it, a little brick post office after that, followed by a clothing shop and a café. "It isn't a big town," Stacy thought, "but it's probably sufficient to serve the ranch community surrounding it."

Pushing the door open, she entered the grocery shop. Behind a narrow counter was a small, matronly lady Stacy guessed to be in her late forties. Her hair was peppered with grey which made her seem more motherly. The simple house dress covering the plump figure reminded Stacy of a kitchen filled with the aromas of fresh-baked cakes. When the customer the woman was waiting on left, Stacy stepped forward.

"Excuse me, are you Mrs. Nolan?"

"Yes, I am. Is there something I could help you with?" the woman asked.

"I'm Stacy Adams. I made arrangements to rent your cabin for the summer," Stacy explained, smiling at the jovial face.

"Of course, how silly of me. I should have recognized you right off. We don't have many tourists stop in our store. You did say you'd be here on the first part of May, but it had completely slipped my mind," apologized the older woman. "I imagine you're anxious to get out there before dark."

"Yes, I had hoped to stay there tonight, Mrs. Nolan."

"Oh, goodness, call me Molly or I'll think you're talking to someone else," she laughed. "My husband will be here shortly and can drive out with you. We cleaned it all up last week, but it's still a little barren. You know how men are, if they got somethin' to sit on and a place to cook food, it don't matter if there's curtains at the windows or a cloth on the table."

"I'm sure it will be fine. I hope you didn't go to too much trouble just for me," answered Stacy, recognizing that the woman had noticed her city clothes and was concerned that Stacy was expecting something fancier.

"Excuse me," a voice from behind Stacy said.

As she turned to move away from the counter, she found herself face to face with the broad shoulders of the stranger from the petrol station. Involuntarily her eyes rushed up to meet his. There was no flicker of recognition in the dark eyes, no spark of interest.

"Oh, Cord, I'm so glad you're here," said Molly Nolan, coming around the counter to take his arm. A faint smile tickled the corners of his mouth as he looked down on the motherly figure. "I want you to meet Miss Stacy Adams. She's rented the hunting cabin in the foothills of the east range for the summer. Stacy, this is Cord Harris, your official landlord. The Circle H headquarters is about ten miles from the cabin.''

Surprised by the unexpected encounter with the stranger a second time, Stacy murmured a polite reply to the introduction and managed to raise her eyes to meet his stony gaze again. This time there was no doubting the hostility and contempt in his eyes. Deliberately they searched her face and continued their way over her yellow top to her creased slacks and fashionable buckle shoes, before returning derisively to her face. The pant-suit that Stacy decided as being practical for travelling before suddenly seemed too chic, too elegant for this rough country.

Embarrassed, she felt the growing heat burning her cheeks. Angry that this Cord Harris had managed to make her feel artificial and cheap, she thrust out her chin defiantly.

''I hope you won't find our country too desolate and isolated for you,'' the man went on, a trace of sarcasm in his voice.

''I'm sure I'll enjoy my stay here. Almost everyone has made me feel very much at home,'' Stacy replied, attempting to curb the anger that trembled on the edge of her words.

''I'm sure they have,'' inserted Mrs. Nolan. ''We don't have many pretty young things like you around here. Why, once the word gets around that you're staying for the summer, our young men will beat a path to your door!''

''I doubt that,'' Stacy smiled, ''but it's nice of you to say so.''

"Not worried about staying alone at that deserted shack, are you?" Cord Harris interposed. "After a few nights alone out there, you'll probably welcome the company of our young men."

"It's possible, but unlikely. You see, Mr. Harris," Stacy was now indignant at the veiled cynicism, "I came here to be alone. I do intend to make friends, but I don't intend to enter the social set."

"'Intend,' very cleverly stated," the dark-haired man drawled, meeting Stacy's flashing eyes with a cool gaze. "It leaves you wide open to do whatever you please. And somehow you don't seem the type to isolate yourself for any amount of time."

"Now, Cord," Molly Nolan put in, trying to quench the unexpected friction between the two. "I don't think it's our place to judge Miss Adams or her plans. You apologize for your rudeness."

"If what I said was unfounded, I certainly do apologize." His hand touched his hat brim, mockingly. "I do hope you enjoy your stay here, Miss Adams, however long it may be."

Nodding a good-bye to Mrs. Nolan, the arrogant rancher picked up his sack of goods and went out the door without allowing Stacy time to reply. Her fury had reached the peak where words failed her. Never had she met such an overbearing, insolent, and sarcastic man! Turning to the astonished woman beside her, Stacy vented her displeasure.

"Who does that man think he is?"

"Oh, you mustn't mind Cord," soothed Molly absently. "He has a tendency to voice his opinion. Underneath all that bluster though, he's really quite charming.''

"You could have fooled me," Stacy exclaimed. "I wish he lived ten thousand miles away instead of just ten. What in the world did I do to warrant such an attack?"

"Nothing, dear, I'm sure. Maybe you just reminded him of someone else," the woman replied bustling around to the other side of the counter. "I imagine you'll want to do some shopping. My husband ought to be here any time now."

Still fuming inwardly, Stacy took a trolley and started down one of the aisles. "He may be my nearest neighbour," Stacy thought, "but I'll make a special point to avoid him from now on, though I would like to see that infuriating coolness of his upset once!"

After picking up all the supplies she felt she would need, Stacy returned to the check-out where she found Molly Nolan engaged in a conversation with a thin, balding man. Guessing that it must be Mr. Nolan, Stacy joined them.

"Well, dearie, did you find everything you needed?" Molly inquired, then turned to the man by her side. "This is Miss Adams, Harry. This is my husband. He'll drive up to the cabin with you."

"I'm happy to meet you, Mr. Nolan," Stacy said, extending her hand to the little man before her.

"Molly said you was a pretty thing, but she didn't say you was this pretty. Ya shore are going to light this little cowtown up," the bright-eyed man replied, eagerly shaking her hand. "I hope the cabin will suit you all right, 'cause it shore ain't very fancy."

"I'm sure it will suit me. I'm used to roughing it with my dad," Stacy said, smiling at the man who was an inch shorter than Stacy's five-foot-four.

"Oh, is your father coming to join you?" Molly asked.

"No." A flicker of pain haunted her face momentarily. "He was killed in a plane crash a month ago."

"Oh, I'm so sorry. I didn't mean to—" Molly started.

"No, you couldn't have known," interrupted Stacy.

"What about your mother? Is she still back East? Does she approve of your gallivantin' off by yourself?" Harry Nolan asked.

"My mother died shortly after I was born, so I'm pretty much on my own now. But you needn't worry about me being alone, I brought my German Shepherd along with me. I'm sure he can handle any four-footed animal that would wander in, and the two-footed variety as well," Stacy laughed, thinking about Cord Harris with a malicious satisfaction.

"Good dogs, them Shepherds," the old man agreed. "He'll watch out for you real good."

"Naturally I hope he won't have to," Stacy said, reaching in her purse to pay for the groceries. "Well, Mr. Nolan, I'm ready to go whenever you are."

"Where'd you park your car?" he asked.

"Across from the drugstore."

"I'll meet ya in about five minutes with my Jeep and you can follow me out," he nodded, moving towards the door.

"Now if you need anything or get to feelin' you want some company, you just hustle yourself into town. Me an' my husband would love to have you any time," said Molly after her husband had left.

"I'll remember. But I think for a while I'm just going to enjoy the peace and quiet," Stacy replied, touched by the motherly concern.

"The folks around here are all pretty friendly and would be more than glad to help you out if you have any kind of trouble, so you just don't hesitate to ask anybody," instructed the matronly woman. "Peace and quiet's fine, but you mustn't shut yourself off completely. You just remember that you're always welcome here and don't be ashamed to ask for help."

"I won't be. Thank you again. You'll be seeing me." Balancing the sack of groceries in one arm, Stacy pushed the door open with the other. It was nice to feel so at home with people she had only met a few minutes ago. With the exception of a certain man, everyone had gone out of his way to help her.

Reaching the car, she put the groceries in the back, quieted the excited dog, and looked around for Mr. Nolan. In the van Diablo was starting to raise a little fuss. Walking back to the trailer, Stacy entered the van by the side door of the empty stall. The sorrel turned his blazed head to her and blew gently on her face. Softly she talked to him, trying to quiet him down. His ears flicked back and forth catching her words, but his eyes still rolled with unease.

Glancing up, Stacy saw Mr. Nolan drive up beside the Jaguar. As she emerged from the van, the wizened old man crawled out of his Jeep and joined her beside the trailer.

"All set to go?" he asked.

"Yes, just making sure everything was secure in the trailer. I'm afraid my horse is a bad traveller," Stacy explained, glancing at the tossing head of the sorrel.

"Mighty flashy-lookin' horse," commented her companion. "What breed is he?"

"Mostly Arabian," Stacy answered, walking over to the driver's side of the sports car.

"Never cared much for them. Too flighty actin'. Give me a steady quarter horse any time," the man answered a little gruffly. "Well, we best get goin'. The road's not in too bad a shape, so you should be able to keep up with me easy." He started the Jeep and moved off.

It wasn't at all difficult to follow him. They drove through a few blocks of homes before taking a gravel road heading north from town. The road soon entered the foothills and finally into the mountains themselves. After they had gone about twenty miles, the Jeep turned on to a side road that was little more than a worn track. Stacy refused to let herself dwell on the jolts her Jaguar was taking and prayed that the low-slung sports car wouldn't get hung up in one of the ruts, while she was trying to concentrate on the bouncing rear end of the Jeep in front of her. She glanced in the mirror anxiously at the horse trailer behind her. Diablo would really be a bundle of nerves by the time she got to the cabin.

The pine woods were so thick that she couldn't see to either side and with the sun setting, the rays filtered through the trees only in patches. The trees thinned out ahead as she watched the vehicle in front go down a small hill into what looked like a clearing. Reaching the top of the hill, Stacy saw a luscious green meadow before her with a stream cascading through it. Off to her left against the back of a canyon wall was nestled a small wooden cabin with a corral and lean-to beside it. Looking to her right briefly, Stacy could see the mountain meadow wander into the arroyos beyond. Why, it was a valley, but more beautiful than any picture she had ever seen.

Harry Nolan had parked his Jeep and was standing by the wooden porch of the cabin when Stacy pulled her black sports car to a stop in front.

"It's beautiful!" she exclaimed, as she got out of the car to gaze at the surrounding mountains.

"Yep," the man replied, removing his straw hat to wipe his balding head with a kerchief. "I'll show you around the inside. I think you'll find it comfortable."

Smiling, Stacy followed the wizened figure into the cabin. The main room housed a fireplace with a large, stuffed deer's head above it. The hearth was filled with firewood with an ample supply piled beside it. There was one sofa in the room and an old rocker. The kitchen, consisting of a few metal cupboards over an old porcelain sink with a pump-type hydrant, covered the west wall. Luckily there was a propane gas stove to cook on; Stacy was sure she could never have managed one of those wood-fired ranges. The table with its two chairs sat in the middle of the room. She could see Molly Nolan's touch in the red-checked tablecloth and matching curtains at the window.

The motherly woman was probably responsible for the pillows on the sofa and the horsehair blanket hanging on the far wall, too. Harry Nolan explained to Stacy how to light the kerosene lanterns and adjust the wick to give off the right amount of light without smoking the glass before he showed her into the bedroom. A big four-poster bed dominated the small room. The bed was covered with a large patchwork quilt that Stacy knew had come from the Nolans. Squeezed in a corner was an old set of chest of drawers. Behind the door was a place to hang her clothes.

"Oh, this is perfect," Stacy smiled, surveying the two rooms excitedly. "I can't think of anything that isn't already here."

"Well, I'm glad it suits you. The missus will be happy to hear how much you like it," said Harry, his bright eyes glowing at Stacy's enthusiasm. "Now, if you'd like, I'll help you unload that horse of yours in the corral."

Accepting Mr. Nolan's offer, Stacy manoeuvred the car so the back of the trailer was over to the gate that the short man had opened. Stacy set the brake and walked back to let the tail gate of the van down before she entered the empty stall beside the restless horse. Anxiously, the sorrel pulled at the rope that held him, interfering with Stacy's attempts to loosen it. She tried to quiet the nervous horse, but his feet increased their tattoo on the trailer's floor as his ears flattened against his head. Finally the knot on the end of the lead rope was loose. As soon as he found himself free, the red stallion half-reared, pulling the girl along with him out of the van. The whites of his eyes flashed menacingly as he danced down the ramp on to the solid ground of the corral. As quickly as she could, Stacy turned the horse loose to gallop around the corral.

The flighty Arabian circled the corral warily, his flaxen mane and tail whipping in the wind. Then his attention was caught by the stranger leaning against the fence rail near his mistress. Instantly he bore down upon the man, his teeth bared and his pointed ears snaked back. With surprising agility the lean man leaped away from the fence and the savage attack.

"Does he do that often?" Harry muttered.

"Fortunately, no," Stacy apologized, waving the horse back to the centre of the pen. "Once in a while he does strike out without any apparent provocation, though."

Studying the spirited horse pacing up and down on the opposite side, head held high into the wind catching the various odours carried by the mountain breeze, Harry turned to Stacy. "What's that scar on his neck? A rope burn?"

"I don't know," she answered, noting the faint white line barely visible under the full mane. "He had it when I bought him."

Eyeing the slim figure speculatively, Harry demanded, "Just how the devil are you able to handle him? He could walk over you like you was air."

"Evidently we have some sort of understanding. Although sometimes I think he just tolerates me," Stacy laughed, shrugging off the concern in the man's voice. Changing the subject quickly, she asked, "Are there many trails around here accessible by horse-back?"

"Plenty. Most of them either lead deeper into the mountains or into the valley, and a few of them branch out over to the Circle H," replied Harry, gesturing towards the west.

"Where is the Circle H exactly?" Her hand shaded her eyes from the setting sun. That was one place she intended to avoid.

"This here's Cord's land that the cabin sits on. We just got a lease. It's an abandoned line shack that me and some of my friends use when we go huntin' and fishin'. But if you're referring to the ranch house, that's about nine, ten miles from here. Yep, he's got himself quite a spread. Runs it with an iron hand, he does. But the men don't mind 'cause they always know where they stand with him. He pays good money and expects a good day's work for it."

Stacy could believe that. He probably rode around with a whip in his hand.

"Molly said you met him at the store," the ageing man added. "'Course, you know he ain't married."

Stacy made no reply as she watched the sorrel paw at some hay in the lean-to. "Who could stand him?" she thought to herself.

"'Bout six years ago, we all thought he'd got himself caught, but the girl up and ran off with some oil-well man. Never did much like the girl. She always thought she was so much better than the folks around here. He's better off without her," nodded Harry, ignoring the bored look on the girl's face, and kept on talking.

Secretly, Stacy couldn't help but applaud the girl who had managed to set that arrogant cowboy back on his heels, but she didn't show it.

"He fixed up his grandma's hacienda on the place for her, piled a lot of money in it. He lives there alone except for his housekeeper." Moving away from the fence, Harry started towards his Jeep. "Well, if I want to get home 'fore dark, I'd better mosey along. If there's anything you need, you be sure to let us know."

"I will, Mr. Nolan. And thanks for all you've done. I really appreciate it," Stacy said, shaking his hand warmly.

She stood in front of the cabin and watched the Jeep drive off on the faint trail into the stand of trees. The solitude encompassed her as she lost sight of the Jeep in the gathering shadows. Cajun came up behind her and shoved his moist nose in her hands. Kneeling down, she rumpled the hair on his neck roughly.

"I'm not alone, am I? Not as long as I have you around, huh?" Stacy smiled, and looked towards the cabin door. "Let's go fix us something to eat."

CHAPTER THREE

THE SUN was streaming over the meadow when Stacy walked out of the cabin door to watch the golden haze cover the meadow. The valley was filled with the songs of birds trilling their greeting to the new day. The sun's rays were striking the rippling brook, turning it into a ribbon of shimmering quicksilver. Inhaling the brisk, clear air, Stacy emitted a satisfied sigh. Then, clicking to the Shepherd standing beside her, she walked over to the corral.

Two days had passed since she had first come to the mountain cabin. The first day Stacy had spent unpacking and settling in. The tack had to be cleaned, as well as the horse trailer and sports car that was dusty from travelling over the gravel roads. She had taken an evening ride down the meadow to give the moody sorrel some exercise and accustom him to the change of climate. The second day she explored the mountains to the east of her, spending most of the day away from the cabin. The scenery continually took her breath away. Never had she travelled so far without finding any trace of civilization except an occasional herd of cattle in the valleys below. Surprisingly enough the evenings had passed rather swiftly for the young girl. After cooking her meal, feeding the horse and dog, she had sat out on the porch until the evening light faded.

It was so restful that, for the first time in several weeks, Stacy felt at peace. Surrounded by the natural serenity of the valley, the worries and grief that had plagued her before seemed non-existent. Nothing mattered but being alive. She knew she had done the right thing in alienating herself from the rest of the world. But part of her never wanted to leave, even though she knew she would have to eventually.

Last evening she had written Carter a letter letting him know she had arrived safely and was settling in. This morning she planned to ride along the main road to find a rancher's mailbox so that she wouldn't have to go into town to post it. She hadn't noticed one on the drive to the cabin, but then she had been concentrating on the road and the vehicle in front of her.

Entering the side gate of the corral near the lean-to, Stacy got the bridle out of the shed and started to approach the red horse who began retreating to the far side of the enclosure. Ignoring the flashing white feet and the small pointed ears that kept flicking back and forth, she walked up to the horse. Snorting, the sorrel lashed out half-heartedly with his front hooves and dashed to the other side of the pen. Arrogantly he looked back at Stacy, tossing his head defiantly.

"All right, Diablo, let's don't play hard to get this morning," Stacy said, walking slowly towards the horse. "It's too lovely a morning to work up a sweat catching you."

The horse stood uneasily as she approached, still talking to him in her soft voice. He eyed her apprehensively as she stopped in front of him and extended her hand. Diablo stretched his small muzzle to her hesitantly and after a little investigation, blew into her hand gently. Docilely he submitted to the bit and bridle and stood quietly, the reins dangling on the ground, while Stacy fetched the blanket and saddle. Stacy never knew how Diablo was going to react to the saddle, sometimes he accepted it calmly and other times he acted like a yearling that had never seen one before. Cinching up, Stacy led the quiet horse out into the yard before mounting. Whistling to Cajun, she started her mount down the trail towards the main road. The sorrel pranced a little as the Shepherd ran alongside, but offered Stacy no trouble.

The sun's rays peeping through the cover of branches danced on the coppery red coat of the horse accenting the whiteness of the rider's blouse. Cajun raced ahead investigating all the sights and sounds of the trail. Acknowledging her sorrel's desire to run, Stacy nudged the horse into a canter. They continued at a ground-eating lope until they reached the main road. Here Stacy slowed the horse to a trot, turning him in the direction of town. Diablo resented the slowed pace and began side-stepping and pulling his head in an attempt to loosen the tight rein. She was unable to admire the scenery as she fought to control her horse. Cajun still led the way, but checked back to make sure his mistress was with him. Stacy's whole attention was devoted to her mount that had begun to rear and plunge around. It was then that she noticed the saddle slipping. The cinch had loosened during the ride from the cabin.

Pulling the horse to a stop, she dismounted. But Diablo had abandoned the earlier docility at the cabin and refused to let her near him. His white feet lashed out, preventing her from approaching him. Slowly Stacy tried to edge her way up the reins to the horse's head, only to have him pull away with his superior strength. Concentrating on trying to quiet the fractious horse, she didn't hear the car coming down the road behind her until it was within a hundred feet. As she turned to see where the vehicle was, Diablo bolted past her, but was pulled up short by the quick thinking of the girl as she yanked the reins hard, forcing the horse to turn in a half circle.

With the noise of the car and the normal misbehaviour of the animal, the sorrel became completely unmanageable. Ignoring the car that had stopped just a few feet away, Stacy concentrated on preventing the horse from breaking away. With the endless open space before her, she knew she would never be able to catch him once he escaped. In the mood he was in now, he would run for miles before stopping.

From the corner of her eye, Stacy recognized the dark, towering figure that had climbed out of the car and was walking towards her. Of all people it had to be Cord Harris. He was the last one she wanted to see just now.

"Looks like you're having a little trouble, Miss Adams," the low-pitched voice drawled.

"Brilliant observation," Stacy said sarcastically, puffing from the exertion of holding the high-strung animal.

Walking up behind her, the man took the reins out of her hands and motioned for her to move back. At the sight of a stranger on the other end of the reins, Diablo renewed his battle for freedom, but he was no match for the determined man. Dodging the flying hooves, Cord grabbed the cheek strap of the bridle and hauled the horse down on all four feet. Gradually the sorrel settled down, tossing his head and snorting occasionally.

Stacy gazed at the broad, muscular shoulders underneath the tan jacket the man was wearing and watched as he ran his hand down the horse's neck. She couldn't imagine anyone being able to win in a fight with this forceful man. Just then he turned his head and met her searching gaze. As much as she wanted to she couldn't keep from staring into the dark eyes that smouldered with a strange, deep fire. He was the one who broke the silence.

"I would recommend you get yourself another horse. He's more than a slip of a girl can handle."

"Thank you, but I didn't ask for your advice, nor did I ask for your help," Stacy retorted, hating the fact that she was beholden to this man.

"It didn't look to me like you were doing a very good job," he replied coldly, his mouth turning up in a mocking smile. "But then, maybe I had the wrong idea."

"I would have been able to handle him if you hadn't driven up in that noisy thing," she said, gesturing defiantly at the sleek gold and brown Continental behind her, "and worried him more than he already was."

"I didn't realize I needed your permission to drive down a public road," drawled Cord Harris, the sarcasm heavy in his voice as his eyes flashed at her. "If your horse is scared of traffic, perhaps you shouldn't be riding him where he's bound to meet it."

"I'm sorry, I shouldn't have said that," Stacy said bitterly. He had done her a favour and she wasn't exactly behaving properly. "He's a little temperamental sometimes, and this happened to be one of those times."

"I hope they don't happen very often or I'll be finding you lying dead somewhere out on the range the next time he throws you."

"Oh, he didn't throw me," Stacy corrected. "I got off to tighten the cinch."

"Oh," he said, a frown creasing his forehead as he turned to the saddle. "I apologize to your horsemanship, then, because I assumed the two of you had parted company a little more dramatically."

"No," Stacy laughed, "though I admit we have a time or two!"

She walked up to fondle the horse's head while Cord proceeded to tighten the girth on the saddle. Turning back to face the girl, he rested his arm on the saddlehorn. Self-consciously, Stacy felt his eyes on her and turned to meet them, but he turned away quickly before she could read the expression written there. When he looked back, his face revealed nothing of his thoughts and Stacy looked away this time, feeling herself redden under his eyes.

"Where were you heading, any place special?" he asked.

"I was looking for a mailbox," Stacy replied hurriedly, trying to cover the sudden unexplainable blush.

"A mailbox!" Cord laughed scornfully. "Just where did you intend to find a mailbox out here?"

"No, I mean a mailbox for a ranch where the mailman delivers and picks up their mail," defended Stacy, her dislike for the arrogant man returning once more.

"Well, I'm sorry to disillusion you, Miss Adams, but there aren't any between here and town," he said, one side of his mouth curling up in disdain. "You forget that this part of the country lacks a few of the luxuries that city people consider necessities."

"I didn't know," she said hotly, her temper rising, "and I don't think it's very amusing of you to degrade a person because of their ignorance."

"I'm not trying to degrade you," Cord said calmly, unruffled by the fiery figure standing defiantly before him. "I'm merely pointing out that you would be more comfortable if you would go back where you belong."

"Mr. Harris, I don't think it's any of your business where I may or may not belong, and I would appreciate it if you would get out of my way so that I may have the pleasure of bidding you good-bye!"

Glowering down at her from his greater height, Cord Harris seemed about to say something, but clamped his mouth shut in a grim line. Although already regretting her hasty words, Stacy felt compelled to raise her chin to emphasize her stand. They stood glaring at each other for a few minutes and then, without warning, the rancher swooped her up in his arms.

"Allow me the privilege of helping you on your way," he said fiercely, holding her in an iron grip against his chest.

So astounded was she by his action that Stacy didn't even attempt to struggle but lay in his arms, her heart beating wildly. She realized that she was playing with fire, crossing this man. Effortlessly, he deposited her in the saddle of the sorrel, tossing the reins over the horse's head. Catching them, she looked down at his blazing eyes.

"That's what you wanted, wasn't it?" the mocking face said darkly.

Regaining some of her composure, Stacy retorted, "As I said before, Mr. Harris, I didn't ask for your help."

"You'll find people around here don't ask—for anything. If they want to do something, they do it."

Diablo, sensing the tension in the air, began dancing about. Stacy could think of no answer to Cord's cryptic words and felt sure that anything she said would only make the situation worse. She didn't want to incur his wrath again. The consequences were too unpredictable with a man like him. With as much poise as she could muster she reined the sorrel around the imposing figure. She could feel his eyes on her as she urged the horse into a trot back up the road she had just come down. Burning in humiliation, she longed to gallop away from those haunting eyes, but her pride insisted on an orderly retreat.

Stacy had to steel herself to keep from looking back. Finally she heard the car door slam and the motor start. Immediately she kicked the sorrel into a gallop.

She didn't allow the horse to slow down until they had reached the turn-off to the cabin.

By the time the three reached the house, Stacy's humiliation had turned to anger. He had no right to treat her like that! His overbearing manner was outrageous and interfering. He acted as if he had a right to tell her what to do. Fuming, she unsaddled the fidgety horse, flinging the saddle and bridle in the shed with an unusual disregard for their care. She stomped out of the corral, closing the gate vehemently, and continued her pace to the porch of the cabin. The dog sensed the mood she was in and scurried off to a corner of the building under the shade.

Disgustedly, Stacy sat in the chair on the porch and gazed moodily at the quiet meadow. She shuddered as she recalled Cord's arms around her. She could still smell the masculine odour of his cologne that was clinging to her blouse. If only she had struggled or fought with him or done anything instead of just lying so passively in his arms, submitting herself to his will! She could have at least scratched those rugged features or pulled his dark hair. Never again would she allow herself to be so weak-kneed in his presence. If she ever met him again, she vowed, she would tell him exactly what she thought of him.

The serenity of the valley meadow failed to comfort her wounded pride. The peace she had felt earlier in the morning was gone and the inactivity of just sitting only increased her agitation. Finally she rose and entered the cabin. It was almost noon, but she had no appetite. Grabbing her swim suit, she changed clothes and, with a terrycloth jacket over her shoulder, started down to the brook that ran through the meadow. Perhaps an icy dip in the mountain stream would cool her temper.

Not far from the cabin the stream widened just deep enough and wide enough to enable her to swim. Kicking off her sandals, Stacy dived into the water. Cajun had followed her at a safe distance and settled himself under a shade tree to watch over his mistress. She splashed around for nearly an hour before pulling herself exhaustedly on to the bank. Propping herself up against the tree with Cajun, she lit a cigarette and relaxed. The afternoon sun started making its way across the sky, but still the two sat under the tree. The exertion of her swim had calmed her nerves, but it hadn't taken away the loathing she felt for the arrogant rancher. She toyed with the idea of returning home, but dismissed it quickly when she remembered Cord Harris's mocking smile as he said, "Go back where you belong." Never would Stacy give him that satisfaction.

"We're going to stay, Cajun, and what's more, we're going to enjoy ourselves. No more are we going to avoid Mr. Harris's ranch. If he doesn't like it, well then, that's just too bad," asserted Stacy, rising to her feet. "Tomorrow, though, I'd better go into town and post that letter before Carter sends a search party after us."

The two started back for the cabin, Cajun trotting contentedly behind the heels of his mistress. Stacy's spirits rose as she walked. Her stride had a little spring in it and her face wore a satisfied expression. She was convinced that any future confrontation with Cord Harris would not find her coming out second best.

THE NEXT morning Stacy overslept, awakening at the persistence of the Shepherd's nuzzling. Hurriedly she had dressed and made coffee. She had hoped to get an early start into town. Just as quickly she fed the dog and gave the sorrel some oats and fresh hay before donning the shirt that matched her yellow slacks. Ordering Cajun to stay at the cabin, Stacy hopped into her black Jaguar and started down the trail to the main road.

She increased her speed, as she turned towards town. This time she was able to look a little more at the view around her. The tall stone mountains seemed to rise out of the prairie as they reached for the sky, their peaks changing into a dark grey contrasting the tans and greens of the plains below. The panoramic view was breathtaking. An occasional greasewood tree dotted the horizon with an exclamation point.

As the car passed the bend in the road where Stacy had had her run-in with Cord Harris yesterday, its speed increased perceptibly. Stacy didn't want to be reminded of that episode and was glad that she could hurry by it. But her spirits were dampened by merely passing the place, causing her to ignore the scenery and concentrate on the road. It was difficult to escape the image of those dark, compelling eyes that had watched her so intently as she sat astride her horse the day before. Their sardonic gleam remained indelible on her memory along with the tanned, sculptured face and dark, almost black hair.

A little over a half hour went by before Stacy reached the town of McCloud. The streets were fairly quiet with only a few people walking from store to store. She parked her sports car in front of the post office. As she climbed out of the car she removed the letter from her purse before walking into the brick building. Nodding a good morning to the clerk in the mail room, Stacy dropped her letter in the outgoing mail slot. She started to leave and then hesitated. Turning around, she walked back to the counter in the mail room.

"Excuse me, is there any mail here for Stacy Adams?" she inquired.

"You're the young lady that rented Nolan's hunting lodge, aren't you?" the quiet voice drawled. "Yes, you had a letter, but I gave it to Cord to drop off to you. You've met him, haven't you? He said he knew you and since he's your neighbour, it seemed natural."

"You gave *him* my letter?" Stacy was astounded. "He knew I would be coming into town."

"Maybe it just slipped his mind," offered the middle-aged man. "He'll probably drop it over to the cabin today. People are pretty neighbourly around here."

"In the future, please hold my mail here until I come personally to pick it up," Stacy said, checking her rising temper. The clerk had obviously thought he was doing her a favour, so she really couldn't blame him.

"Yes, ma'am," he replied, eyeing her quizzically.

With a quiet thank-you, Stacy turned away from the counter and walked out the door. Reaching the sidewalk, she stopped and hesitated for a minute. She decided that it would only be polite to stop in and talk to Mrs. Nolan and thank her for all the extra work she had gone to at the cabin.

As she walked into the grocery store, she noticed Molly talking to a young, red-haired woman with two spirited youngsters tugging at her skirt. When Mrs. Nolan recognized Stacy coming in, her face immediately broke into a smile that reached all the way to her eyes. The young woman beside her also turned to meet Stacy. Her smile held as much welcome as Molly Nolan's.

"Stacy, I was wondering how you were gettin' along," the elder woman said, walking up to take both of Stacy's hands in her own. "Cord said he met you on the road yesterday and you seemed to think you were doing all right."

"Yes, I'm doing fine," Stacy replied, biting her lip to keep from making a caustic comment about Cord Harris. "And I love the cabin. Mr. Nolan told me about all the decorating you did to make it more feminine, and I want to thank you."

"Well, don't thank just me, thank my daughter, too," Molly said, indicating the redhead beside her. "I'm glad you stopped in, because I was really lookin' forward to you two meetin'. Mary, this is Stacy Adams, as you must have guessed. And this is my daughter, Mary Buchanan."

"I'm so pleased to meet you at last. Mother has talked of nothing else, but that 'lovely young girl' living all alone in the cabin, and she didn't quite do you justice," the young woman smiled, extending a hand to Stacy.

"Thank you," Stacy replied. "Your mother has really made me feel at home."

"I think she'll always be the mother-hen type looking after her chicks regardless of whether they're hers or not," teased Mary, smiling affectionately at the woman beside her. "As you must have guessed, these two Indians here are mine. This is Jeff and this is Dougal."

Stacy knelt down to shake hands with the two young boys.

"You're awful pretty," Jeff said, scrutinizing the golden-brown hair that fell becomingly around the oval face smiling back at him. "'Most prettier than Mom."

"Well, thank you," Stacy laughed.

"You have conquered him," Mary smiled, gazing at her oldest son with pride. "But then he always had good taste. Takes after his father."

"Naturally," said Molly, "and don't ever forget it!"

"That's Mom, always reminding me what a catch I made, as if I would forget," Mary grinned. "Are you in a hurry or anything? Why don't you come over to my house for coffee?"

"That would be wonderful," said Stacy, warming to the friendliness of the attractive woman. "My car's parked right out front and—"

"Good, we walked down here and now we can beg a ride back," Mary said with a bewitching smile. "We only live a few blocks away."

"You two run along then," said Molly Nolan, "so I can get back to work. Take care of these two boys. And don't let them eat all that candy I gave them."

Mary directed Stacy to her home, a beautiful ranch-type house with a large fenced yard. The boys brawled out of the car reluctantly, wishing the ride could have lasted longer.

"They really got a thrill out of riding in your car. They'll remember that for ages," said Mary, opening the front door and waiting for Stacy to enter first.

"I enjoyed it, too," Stacy answered as she followed the other girl into a big, spacious kitchen. "As trite as it sounds, I love children."

"Well, I'm not going to make that natural comeback of 'wait until you have some of your own,' because I love mine and wouldn't change them for the world," Mary agreed, heating coffee for the two of them. "Mothers that moan and groan about all the trouble their children make almost drive me up the walls."

"I know what you mean, although I'm not too experienced on the subject," Stacy said, sitting down at the table.

"Tell me, do you have someone waiting back home?"

"Sort of," said Stacy, remembering Carter Mills and his recent proposal.

"Sort of? You mean, he hasn't popped the question and you've come out here to make him see how much he misses you?" Mary concluded as she joined Stacy at the table with the coffee. "Cream or sugar?"

"No, black," Stacy answered. "He did propose before I left, but I'm not sure if I want to get married just yet."

"Do you love him?"

"I suppose so. I've never dated anyone else but him. We just knew each other so well that—"

"I see what you mean," Mary nodded. "I suppose with the loss of your father and all, you didn't want to make any rash decisions."

"Partly," Stacy sighed.

"Maybe being apart will help you decide how much you really do care for him," suggested Mary, realizing that the girl beside her was confused. "Fortunately, there never was any doubt for me as to how I felt about Bill. He's the doctor here. The minute he got into town and took over old Doc Gibbon's practice, I knew he was the man I wanted to marry. I was almost twenty-two by then and had dated my share of men."

"I wonder if that's my problem. Travelling with my father on his various photography assignments the way I did, I was never in any one place long enough to meet people my age." It was comforting to be able to confide in Mary, a comparative stranger. "And when I got back to town I always had Carter to fall back on. I admit I did have a crush on one of the reporters Dad worked with," Stacy chuckled.

"I guess everyone has those," Mary laughed. "I had it bad for Cord Harris. I used to chase him all over."

"Cord Harris?"

"Yes. Every girl around here has fallen under his spell at one time or another. He used to be quite the playboy,'' said Mary, a smile playing at the corners of her mouth.

"That woman-hater? I can't imagine him being polite to anyone!" commented Stacy.

"I assure you he's not a woman-hater. He's a little bitter after that dirty deal Lydia Marshall pulled on him. But it's only a matter of time before some girl breaks through that thin veneer of his, and then you'll see what I'm talking about. When he turns the charm on, nobody is immune," Mary concluded with a shake of her titian hair.

"You're looking at one girl who is immune," Stacy said vehemently. "He is beyond doubt the most arrogant, despicable man I've ever had the misfortune to meet!"

"I see he's made a distinct impression on you." Mary hid a smile with difficulty. "I think you may have judged him a little too quickly. Ignoring his superb good looks and his great six-foot-four frame, you'll still find he has all the requirements of a good husband and father. And if that isn't enough, he owns the biggest ranch around and runs it with a profit."

"That's all well and good, but I still pity the woman that ever marries him. He didn't hesitate to form a hasty opinion of me, and I don't intend to turn the other cheek."

"Whew! The sparks must fly when you two get together," Mary exclaimed, amused and puzzled. "Funny, I thought you two would hit it off rather well."

"Well, we don't," Stacy said, hoping to close the subject. She couldn't bring herself to confide in this

understanding girl about yesterday's episode. The
humiliation was too fresh in her mind to talk about.

It was the middle of the afternoon before she bade
the friendly family good-bye and promised to stop the
next time she came to town.

In less than an hour, the young girl was back at her
cabin being greeted by the wildly thumping tail of the
Shepherd. Happily the two entered the cabin. While
Stacy was preparing their supper, she noticed a note on
the table. Walking over to pick it up, she saw an envelope underneath it. Quickly she read the note.

"So sorry I missed you," it read. "I took the
liberty of bringing your mail.

C.H."

"The nerve of that man!" Stacy said aloud, rip-
ping the note into shreds and throwing it into the fireplace. "'So sorry I missed you.' Hmph!" she
muttered, returning to the stove. "Well, I'm not!"

After eating, she took her coffee out to the porch
and read the letter from Carter in the waning light.

CHAPTER FOUR

THE LATE afternoon sun cast a long shadow of horse and rider picking their way through the rocky foothills. The red horse pranced a little as a lizard darted across their path, but responded to the quiet words from the rider on his back. From an arroyo on their left came the German Shepherd to rejoin his mistress.

Stacy called a hello to the dog and urged the horse into a canter on to the opening flatland. A smile rose on her lips as she turned to survey her backtrail with satisfaction. To her there could be nothing as beautiful as this untamed land. She was glad she had finally decided to trespass on the Circle H home range. The scenery was fantastic in its undisciplined beauty. Pulling the stallion up near some greasewood bushes, she dismounted to sit in their shade and gaze at the panoramic view before her.

After removing the flat gaucho hat, she dusted her white blouse off. They had been exploring since midmorning and even though she could feel the tiring of her muscles, she was still exhilarated by the wonderful country she had seen. She glanced at her watch and knew that when she remounted she would have to go directly back to the cabin in order to make it before sundown. After dark she might have trouble finding her way back.

Her thoughts turned to the letter she received yesterday from Carter. She knew he wouldn't be so eager for her to return if he were here beside her to enjoy all this scenery. And return she would have to. She couldn't cut herself away from the rest of the world indefinitely. Nature in all its harsh beauty had brought this realization to her today. She had decided during her ride that she would return in two or three weeks. This would be her vacation. She was sure that was the way her father would have wanted it. She'd get a job somewhere, maybe in a travel bureau. If not she would find something else.

But marriage? No, she wasn't ready for that, she thought as she shook her head. She cared too much for Carter to grab at the straw of escape he offered her. When they married, or rather when she married, Stacy knew she wanted to put her whole heart into it and the family that would come. She could only hope that Carter would understand that she wanted herself whole again before they made any life together.

Standing up, she faced the gentle breeze ruffling her long hair and smiled as she inhaled the fresh air. Life was good and there wasn't any sense in worrying about things that hadn't happened. Crossing over to the sorrel, she picked up the reins. Remounting, she whistled to the dog and turned her horse into the mountains from which they had come.

The horse broke into an eager trot, refreshed by the brief rest in the meadow. Stacy captured his spirit and eased her hold on the reins. The horse immediately moved into a rocking lope. As they reached the rock-strewn foothills, his gait slowed to a fast walk as he picked his way. Cajun followed not far behind. Stacy turned for one last look at the grassland she had left.

At that moment, with Stacy turned and off-balance in the saddle, a rattlesnake resting underneath a nearby bush sounded his warning. Before Stacy could turn around, Diablo was screaming, rearing high into the air. His terror was beyond restraint as he shook his head violently, protesting Stacy's instant tightening of the reins. Spinning in a half rear towards the flatland, the stallion unseated his light rider completely. As Stacy lost her grip and tumbled off, the horse bolted, taking his avenue of escape.

Unable to break her fall, Stacy landed heavily on her shoulders. Her neck snapped back at the impact, striking her head on a rock. Pain seared through her body. Valiantly she attempted to fight the unconsciousness that threatened her. She struggled up on one elbow, catching a glimpse of Diablo streaking across the meadow with his tail high. Vaguely she recognized the Shepherd racing towards her before she succumbed to the promising relief of blackness.

FROWNING, STACY turned slightly to look where the voice had come from. With difficulty she forced her eyes to focus on the smiling face hovering above her.

"Where am I? My father, is he—" she started, her brown eyes glancing around the unfamiliar setting in panic. Then she closed her eyes and added, "I remember now. I fell."

"Don't try to talk," admonished the doctor. "You've had a bad fall, but you're going to be fine. I'm Dr. Buchanan, Mary's husband."

Attempting a smile at the recognized name, Stacy tried to speak. "Is Mary here?"

"No, you're at the Circle H. Cord Harris found you and brought you to his ranch. You owe him a great debt."

"No!" Stacy cried, feebly struggling to rise from the bed. "I can't stay here, I can't!"

"Now listen, young lady," the doctor said, gently restraining her movement. "You need rest. The best place for you right now is in this bed."

Pleadingly she looked into his face, her eyes clouding with tears as she desperately willed him to change his mind. His returning gaze was adamant. Involuntarily her eyes turned to the doorway that was now blocked by Cord. It was impossible to tell how long he had been there, his fierce gaze taking in both parties.

"Oh, why," she sobbed helplessly, "why did you have to be the one who found me?"

"I assure you I wasn't out looking for you," was the caustic reply. "I found your horse running loose and backtracked him."

"That's enough talking," interrupted Dr. Buchanan. "It's time you rested."

Not having the strength to fight either her unwanted host or the doctor's orders, Stacy turned her face from both of them and allowed the frustration and pain to sweep her away. The two men's eyes locked over the girl, the rancher's defiant and unflinching, the other's probing and questioning.

"I think we should leave her to rest in quiet," the doctor suggested, gathering up his instruments.

IT WAS late evening before Stacy woke again. She lay quietly in the bed and studied her surroundings with a little more interest. The bedroom was masculine with heavy Spanish furniture and bold, definite colours. She couldn't help wondering if this was the rancher's bedroom. It seemed stamped with the same austere personality that branded Cord Harris. Dark mahogany beams coursed the ceiling, accenting the white, textured paint. The coarse-grained effect was carried through in the curtains with their loose-weave tweed in reds and oranges that was repeated in the coverlet on her bed.

Stacy pushed herself into a sitting position in the bed, fighting off the wave of nausea that followed the movement. She was wearing a nightgown. The realization shocked her as she looked down at the yellow bodice. How and when had she changed? Who had helped her? Her face crimsoned at the thought of the muscular Texan. It was even her own nightgown. How had he come into possession of it? Unless, of course, he had sent someone after her things. But he wouldn't dare have the nerve to touch her!

"Well, I see you've returned to us. I thought you were going to sleep all through the night," came a low voice from the doorway.

Stacy's eyes snapped up to face her unexpected visitor, her cheeks still blushing. "What time is it?" Stacy stammered, unnerved at seeing the man who had been occupying her thoughts.

"After eight," Cord replied, pulling up a chair beside her bed and gazing at her intently. His voice held no trace of the sarcasm she associated with him as he asked, "How are you feeling?"

"Better," she replied, unable to meet his penetrating eyes. "I want to thank you for all you've done. I—"

"There's no need. I consider myself lucky that I spotted your horse. I hate to think how long you might have lain out there before you were found." His low voice still carried that gentle tone that was so unfamiliar to her and did such strange things to her heart. "Here, let me fix those pillows for you."

Self-consciously Stacy allowed him to add another pillow behind her head. Aware of his nearness, she glanced up to his face, taking in the clear cut of his jaw and soft firmness of his mouth, but refusing to look above the high cheekbones at the dark, unfathomable eyes. She caught the scent of his cologne which she remembered so vividly from their encounter on the road. It was difficult to ignore the muscular chest and arms encased in the crisp white shirt. Stacy was sure he could hear the wild beating of her heart and cursed the way his physical presence could arouse her.

"Isn't that more comfortable?" said Cord, reseating himself in his chair. A smile was showing faintly on his mouth as if acknowledging the girl's embarrassment at his nearness. He couldn't fail to detect the flush growing in her cheeks as she sat silently with downcast eyes. "Perhaps, Stacy, we should try to begin again," he said, his voice changing to an impersonal tone at her continued absorption with a bow on her gown. "We got off to a rather bad start. The doctor feels that it's best for you to stay here until you can get back on your feet. As it will only be a temporary situation, it will make it easier for both of us if we ignore our personal feelings."

Surprised at his open acknowledgement of the unspoken antagonism between them, Stacy looked up into the two dark eyes regarding her so thoughtfully.

"Well, are we friends?"

Hesitantly Stacy placed her slim hand in the outstretched palm. It was engulfed in the large, tanned hand. She felt he held it a little longer than was necessary, yet the suddenness of his release upset her. His brows were now contracted in that old familiar frown and his mouth curled in a whimsical smile as he rose and looked down at her. Once again his size and air of superiority overwhelmed her.

"I imagine you're more interested in getting something to eat than listening to me. I'll send Maria in with some soup and tea," the dark figure said, moving towards the end of the bed. "Oh, by the way, your dog is outside and your horse is bedded down in one of our stud pens. I also took the liberty of bringing a few of your things here from the cabin. I hope you don't mind."

"No," Stacy answered, surprised at the meekness in her voice.

"Good," he said, a twinkle now in his eyes. "In case you were wondering, Maria 'prepared' you for bed."

Indignation rose in her as the tall rancher left the room. "He's positively insufferable!" she thought.

How could she have been taken in by that initial gentleness? Just imagining how he must have been laughing at her all the while he was sitting there angered her further. He was right about one thing—for the time being, she had to compromise until she was on her feet again. The throbbing in her head forced her thoughts to change to quieter things.

By the time the robust housekeeper, Maria, arrived with her food, Stacy's composure had returned, though she was sure her cheeks still retained some of their unnatural colour.

"Ah, the leetle one is feeling much better, no?" smiled the jovial Mexican, placing the tray with a steaming bowl of broth on Stacy's lap. "The head, eet does not hurt so much?"

"Only a little. The soup smells good," Stacy replied, inhaling the invigorating aroma of the hot broth. She was hungrier than she had thought. Thankfully Maria left the room and Stacy was allowed to eat at her leisure. She had just finished the last of the tea when the Mexican woman returned for the tray.

"That was very good, Maria," Stacy smiled, handing the tray to the waiting hands.

"*Gracias.* I cook good. Meester Cord, he say my cooking the best anywhere in Texas." The large woman giggled at the audacity of the claim.

"Well, perhaps he exaggerated a little, but it was very good," Stacy laughed.

"You get some more sleep now," Maria instructed, helping Stacy settle back under the covers. "We have you up in no time. Doctor say for you to keep warm and rest, but thees bed so beeg you get lost in it. I tell Meester Cord, but he say eet all right. Pooh! You should have a man to keep you warm, not a beeg bed.''

Stacy could feel herself blushing at the woman's advice. She remembered again her impression that this was Cord's bedroom. She had to ask.

''*Si, si,*'' the big woman laughed. ''You theenk maybe he sleep here tonight. No, he thought eet better he sleep in office.''

Maria continued her laughing, her belly rolling with the force of her mirth and her fatty underarms bouncing as she carried the tray out of the room. Stacy glanced apprehensively around before putting out the light. Although fearful that she would be unable to sleep, she dropped off almost immediately.

THE MORNING sun was dancing its patterns on the braided rug beside Stacy's bed. Maria had already brought in her breakfast and had helped her clean up. Rather than attempting to brush the hair around her wound, Stacy had merely pulled it back and tied it with a bow to match the bedjacket that had been brought along with her other clothes. She felt much better as long as she ignored the dull pain in her head and the sniffles in her nose. She was just examining the unusual scrollwork in the bedroom door when it opened to admit the smiling face of Cord Harris.

''Good morning. Maria said you were up.'' His low voice was cheerful with no trace of sarcasm. ''Do you feel like a visitor?''

''A visitor?'' Stacy echoed, trying to think of who would be coming to see her. ''Yes.''

"Okay, feller, come on in," said Cord, swinging the door wider to admit a cautious German Shepherd.

"Cajun!" Stacy exclaimed happily as the big dog recognized the figure in the bed and bounded to her, his tail wagging happily. With his front paws on the bed, he proceeded to give her a thorough washing with his big tongue. "Stop it, you silly idiot!"

"I think he's rather pleased to see you. He refused to eat this morning and wouldn't move away from the front door, so I decided the best thing would be to let him see for himself that you were all right," Cord explained still standing in the doorway.

"I hope he wasn't too much of a bother," Stacy said after she had managed to push the Shepherd off the bed and on to the floor where he sat gazing at his mistress with undisguised adoration. "I'm afraid we're rather attached to each other."

"I have some work to do around the ranch, so I'll leave the dog here for company. I've instructed Maria to bring you some books from the library. I know we don't have the elegant surroundings you've been accustomed to, but if there's anything else you would like, just ask and we'll see what we can arrange."

"Thank you," she replied, wishing she could think of something else to say. "Everything's fine, really, and I'll try not to be any trouble to you."

"You won't be—at least, not any more than I can handle," he replied. The mocking smile returned to his face before Cord left, closing the door behind him.

"Have you ever been 'handled' before?" Stacy asked the Shepherd, wondering why Cord had developed such a negative attitude towards her. "I imagine he thinks he can 'handle' anything that comes along!"

A few minutes later Maria arrived with some novels and magazines. Stacy noticed a couple of her favourite books and settled back to read. The day passed rather swiftly. With each knock on the door she half expected to see the rancher appear. When Maria returned for the supper tray that evening and Cord still hadn't come, Stacy decided that he wasn't going to come. Strangely enough, she felt disappointed. She tried to attribute it to her loneliness and desire for company regardless of how arrogant he might be.

CHAPTER FIVE

WITH A contented sigh, Stacy rested her head against the cushion and gave the Shepherd lying beside her an affectionate pat. Her soft brown curls lay carelessly around her neck, touching the edge of the simple orange and yellow shift with its V-neck and capped sleeves. Her tanned legs glistened all the way down to the Roman sandals she wore.

A subtle application of powder hid the slight redness around her straight nose that was the last reminder of the cold that had racked her body with chills and fever the past week. Her recovery had been swift, thanks to the quick action of Dr. Buchanan who had been summoned as soon as the course of her illness became apparent, and had given her medication.

Stacy was so engrossed in her outdoor surroundings that she failed to hear the measured steps entering the cobblestoned veranda until they were a few feet from her. Instantly she recognized the deliberate walk; hadn't she listened for it enough times outside her bedroom door this past week? It belonged to Cord Harris. Looking up, she met the full gaze of the rugged man's dark eyes. Her own travelled over the blue turtle-necked shirt accenting his broad shoulders and muscular arms, then down the trim waist and narrow hips, taking in the black slacks tapering over his dress boots.

So accustomed was she to seeing Cord in ranch wear, Stacy was surprised that he wore the dressy sports clothes with such ease. Most outdoor men she had met always looked uncomfortable in anything other than their everyday wear. She couldn't help noticing that there was no tell-tale sunburn where the hat brim ended nor where the sleeve of his shirt started. He obviously found time to make use of the pool.

Uncomfortably aware that she had been staring, Stacy blushed. A tall glass of iced liquid was held before her by a large, tanned hand. Timidly she accepted it, and her half-raised eyes caught the bemused smile on Cord's face. Though he had noticed Stacy's scrutinizing stare, Cord made no comment as he pulled up a rattan chair beside her.

"You're looking very well," he said gently, his eyes flicking over her face. "I hope the drink is satisfactory. I don't know if it's included in the doctor's orders, but it can't do any harm."

"Thank you. It's fine," Stacy replied, taking a sip out of the tall glass. Her senses were tingling with the nearness of her host as the smell of shampoo and shaving lotion wafted over to her in the evening breeze.

"I imagine it feels rather good to get outside after being shut in for so long."

"Yes, it does. You have such a beautiful view. You must be exceptionally proud of your home," said Stacy, a nervous lilt in her voice. She felt an unaccountable need to keep the conversation going.

"The antiqueness of the hacienda doesn't offend you?"

"Oh, no!" she exclaimed, her eyes widening. "It's lovely. You must have done a lot of remodelling."

"Yes, we did. The original hacienda enclosed this area here. It served as a fortress against attacks in the early days. When I decided to remodel it, I eliminated the south and west wings. Even now there's more room than a bachelor needs," Cord informed her with a smile.

"But when you marry and have children, it will be perfect," Stacy said as she looked at the whitewashed adobe walls.

"Undoubtedly." There was a coldness and withdrawal in his tone and his attention was riveted on a distant mountain.

"What I meant was the size—" she stammered.

"I understand what you mean, Miss Adams," returning his dark, expressionless eyes to her. "But I don't anticipate that prospect being fulfilled in the near future."

Obviously he was referring to his star-crossed romance with the girl Mary had spoken about. "You never know," Stacy replied a little more brightly than she felt. "I'm sure there are a lot of girls who are very anxious to change your mind, Mr. Harris."

"Are you one?" A raised eyebrow disappeared into the black hair curling over his forehead.

"I wasn't referring to myself," she replied a trifle indignantly.

"It's very romantic-sounding to marry a man who owns a spread the size of this one, but reality is quite another thing," he continued. "This is a hard, demanding land even in these advanced times. The hours are long and the results are unpredictable at best. A wife can expect to be alone a great deal, and isolated. As far as entertainment is concerned, it's non-existent with the exception of an occasional social gathering. The same with the large department stores you're accustomed to. Major shopping requires a trip to San Antoine or El Paso. The rigours of this life are more than a city girl would want to cope with."

"I wasn't applying for the position, Mr. Harris," Stacy retorted, rising from the chaise with a reddened face.

"Cord," he supplied, towering over her as he rose. Taking her arm, he steered her towards the pool, his eyes sparkling with amusement. "Come over here. I want to show you something."

"What is it?" Her impatience was marked by the sharpness in her voice.

"Really, Miss Adams," Cord said in a mock scolding voice. "I would have thought you'd learned by now how to take a little teasing!"

"I have met certain egotistical men who would be vain enough to believe that all women fall at their feet!"

"As I have met women who feel they're the answer to every man's prayer and he should succumb to their charms." The two had reached the opposite side of the pool and stood facing each other defiantly, his hand still upon her arm. The air between them crackled with the unspoken challenge. His voice was low as he turned to face the horizon. "Continuing this subject would accomplish nothing. We both have our own views.''

"Precisely," Stacy said crisply. "Now if you'll show me whatever it is you wanted me to see, I'll return to my room."

"You wouldn't be interested."

"What was it?" Stacy asked, slightly curious despite her annoyance with the arrogant man.

"Only an old family cemetery. I'm sure some ancient gravestones wouldn't interest your sophisticated tastes," Cord replied sarcastically, his back now turned to her.

"I would like to see it."

"It's not necessary," he answered, as if this was an attempt at an apology on Stacy's part.

"Mr. Harris, the last thing I would do is go to patronize you. You said earlier that we should bury the hatchet and be friends. Obviously your wounded ego can't comprehend anything but undying loyalty. Now I would like to see 'your' cemetery. If you don't want to accompany me, tell me where it is and I'll go by myself."

The biting tone of her voice turned Cord towards her, his cool eyes examining her face as if assuring himself of her genuine interest.

"It's only a little way from here, but it's uphill. I wouldn't want you to overdo it your first time out. Perhaps we should postpone it." At the angry denial forming on Stacy's lips, Cord went on, "But if you're sure you want to go, I'll go with you."

"I'm sure."

"Very well."

He started to take her arm again, but Stacy shrugged him off and began walking in the direction he had indicated. Cord followed a step or two behind as they made their way up the knoll behind the house. The incline was slight, but in Stacy's weakened condition she found herself out of breath when they reached the top. She managed to ignore the sardonic gleam in Cord's eyes and pushed on towards the wrought iron enclosure ahead.

The assorted crosses and gravestones were dwarfed by a large monument in the centre. Years had weathered most of them, but Stacy noticed that the area was well kept. The grillework, which should have rusted from age, still had a certain freshness in its black exterior and the ground had been seeded with grass, its green blanket lovingly covering the graves in a spring shroud. Cord opened the gate and Stacy walked inside.

The two walked silently on the trodden path around the dozen headstones before coming to a stop near the centre. Most of the dates were in the late 1800s and early 1900s. Four of the smaller crosses marked children's graves. One stone was recent, dated eight years ago and bore the words "Stephen Harris—Father."

"Is that your father's grave?" Stacy asked quietly, the word "father" bringing a melancholy to her voice as the freshness of her own loss washed over her.

"Yes."

"I didn't notice your mother's. Is she buried here?"

A shadow passed over his face as Cord replied, "She's buried back East with her family." There was a briskness in his voice and a hardness in his eyes.

"She couldn't stand the ranch and its demands on her and my father. A few years after I was born she went back to her family."

"She left you?" Stacy asked, pity in her heart for the now dead man and his abandoned son.

"Father gave her no choice," Cord said, his steel black eyes on her face, rejecting the sympathy he saw. "I doubt if you'd understand. This is a hard land. You must take what is yours and then fight to keep it. My mother was a pampered child used to being waited on, so the future that was offered meant nothing to her. She wanted the luxuries she was accustomed to and her demands never stopped, not on my father's attention or his money. There wasn't enough of either for her."

"And the ranch came first," Stacy murmured astutely.

"Do you see this marker here?" Cord asked, turning to the centre monument. "Elena Teresa Harris, my grandmother. She was a Spanish aristocrat who fell in love with my grandfather, who was a struggling rancher at that time with a lot of dreams. She was a real woman. He had nothing to offer her but an old adobe three-room house, a few head of cattle and a lot of land that was dry most of the time. But it didn't matter to her."

There was no denying the respect and admiration in his voice as he spoke. Momentarily he stepped forward and opened the gate for Stacy, following her out. Engrossed in their conversation, she accepted his hand on her arm as they walked to the edge of the knoll looking down on the ranchyard below. With his other hand, Cord pointed towards the western mountains, purpled in the twilight.

"The Mescalero Apaches used those mountains as a stronghold and raided settler and small ranchers at will. And the 'Comanche War Trail' is not far from here either. At the turn of the century the Indian raids had ended and this western region was populated by cattlemen seeking these rich pastures where grass was so abundant. Most of the settlers ran more cattle than the land could support—overgrazed it. That's why there's so much desert land out here today."

"Can't it be reseeded? Left alone to grow back?" There was concern in Stacy's upturned face.

"It's too late for most reclamation. Either the wind carries the seed away, or the rain doesn't come when it's needed, or it washes the seed away before it gets a chance to deepen its roots. Ignorance and greed do more damage to the future than they do to the present," Cord answered grimly. "But my father and grandfather realized this. In more than one way, I have them to thank for what I have today."

"You must be very proud of them," Stacy said with a smile. "A lot of things have changed since your grandfather's time."

"He was a cattleman, tried and true. He'd turn over in his grave if he saw sheep grazing on his land," Cord chuckled.

"Sheep?" Astonishment was written on Stacy's face. "You raise sheep?"

"Yes, I have a few hundred head of registered stock on the higher pastures."

"You don't run them with the cattle?"

"Sometimes, usually in the summer when we move the cattle to the foothills. We also have some Angora goats, but they're in the experimental stages as far as our ranch is concerned. Quite a number of ranchers have had good success with them. And there's our quarter horses. We have two exceptional studs and several young breeding prospects. I've doubled the number of brood mares in the home herd. We have an auction on the grounds every spring, selling some of the yearlings and two-year-olds that we aren't going to keep or older brood mares we want to replace with new blood."

"I didn't realize you had so many individual enterprises," Stacy mused, awed by the size of the ranch's operation. "I suppose there are oil wells, too."

"No civilized Texas ranch would be complete without them," Cord laughed quietly at the dazed expression on his companion's face. "We have four on the east boundary. Only two are still in operation. Most all of the ranch property is outside of the oil-producing region."

"I'm beginning to understand what the expression 'cattle baron' means," Stacy commented, looking up at the bronze face.

"Don't let the magnitude of all of it lull you into thinking it's an easy life," he warned her. "As diversified as the ranch has grown, it's only increased the work load and the difficulty of control."

Stacy grimaced at his words. It was hard to imagine this powerful man not in control. He was so sure of what he wanted that nothing would dare stand in his way.

"Looks like Dr. Buchanan's car driving in," Cord went on, watching a station wagon pull up behind the house below. "We'd better go down. Maria will probably have dinner ready shortly, anyway."

Nodding her agreement, Stacy followed him down the slope. By the time they reached the veranda, the smiling face of the young doctor was there to greet them. To Stacy's pleasant surprise, his wife Mary had accompanied him. The happy red-haired woman walked forward, arms outstretched to the younger girl.

"You look marvellous!" Mary exclaimed, clasping Stacy's hands warmly in hers. "Tell me, Stacy, how have you two been getting along?" she teased in a low voice. "I don't see any battle scars."

"Cord and I have buried the hatchet, haven't we?" Stacy replied with a throaty laugh. Glancing at the tall figure standing beside the doctor, she continued, "We found some common ground that we both agree upon."

Only the rancher understood the oblique reference to their earlier dialogue about their opinions of each other. Coolly she met his dark eyes, keeping the smile off her lips with difficulty. But in Mary's matchmaking mind, a totally different conclusion was reached.

"Well, this is news," Bill Buchanan remarked. "The last time I was here, Stacy, you couldn't wait to leave." With a grin on his boyish face, he added to Cord, "Maybe my patient's suffering a relapse."

"I think she's just recognizing some of the attractions that can be found here," Cord replied, quirking his mouth into a smile. "With a girl as pretty as Stacy,

I'll have to act as a guide myself to keep the young men from falling under her spell.''

Stacy caught the emphasis on her name, realizing he had noticed she had used his Christian name for the first time. Deliberately she met his mocking gaze and taunting words.

Stacy couldn't explain, even to herself, why she had referred to the angry words they had had before. She had enjoyed the easy companionship on the hill and the informative talk. Why had she taunted him? Did she feel safer with his mocking words and sarcastic smile? Pointedly she turned the conversation to Mary's two children. Several times she felt Cord's eyes searching her face, but she deliberately avoided looking at him.

"I'm afraid we're rather poor hosts, Cord," she murmured, trying to cover the confusion he was causing by standing so close to her. Unaccountably, her hand drifted on his arm. "We didn't offer the doctor and Mary something to drink."

There was a darting look of surprise in Cord's eyes as he looked at the upturned face, but it was quickly suppressed by a smile to his guests. Guiltily she dropped her hand.

"I'll have Maria bring us something. Anything special you'd like, Bill, Mary?"

"No," Bill laughed. "Anything tall and cool will do."

Cord left them for a moment to arrange for the refreshments. During that time Mary and her husband seated themselves in two of the garden chairs while Stacy settled on the cushioned settee. A few minutes later Cord returned followed by the plump Mexican woman carrying a tray laden with drinks and hors d'oeuvres. To Stacy's chagrin, Cord sat on the settee with her. Her annoyance escaped the other couple's attention amidst the confusion of accepting the refreshments Maria offered, but the one-sided smile on Cord's lips indicated that he had noticed her dismay.

To Stacy's relief, the conversation remained on a light vein. Several times she was uncomfortably aware of the dark brown eyes studying her and the magnetic closeness of the outstretched arm on the back of the couch. Mary, with her naturally lively personality, monopolized most of the conversation with anecdotes of the children, but gradually the subject turned to Stacy and her accident.

"When Bill told me that day about your fall, I practically insisted on bringing you into town with us," Mary chattered. "But he assured me it was better to leave you here where you would have ample opportunity to rest."

"Actually what I said was 'peace and quiet'," inserted the doctor with a smile. "That's something hard to come by in our house."

"He's always complaining about the boys," explained Mary, "but he loves them as much as I do. Anyway, I can see how right he was. You look the picture of health. Of course, with this kind of scenery who would want to stay in bed?"

There was a twinkle in Mary's eyes as she gave Cord a sideways glance. Hastily Stacy spoke up, not wanting the innuendo to go any further.

"This is a beautiful ranch," she rushed. "The whole land around here is fascinating. It reminds you what little time has passed since it was a frontier."

"Texas history is fascinating," agreed the blue-eyed doctor.

"Were you at the cemetery when we came?" Mary directed at Cord. Without waiting for his affirmative nod, she continued, "I wish you could have met his grandmother, Stacy. She was a wonderful old woman. You never thought of her as old, though. She was much too vital and active. I was only nine or ten when she died, but I remember her so well."

"Cord told me a little about her," Stacy said.

"She was remarkable. Somewhere amongst all her Spanish ancestry she inherited a pioneer spirit that was indefatigable," Mary went on. "But there was a certain way about her—the way she carried her head or looked deep inside you—that reminded you of her blue blood. My mother always said Doña Elena was the only one able to handle Cord." In a conspiratorial aside to Stacy, she added, "He was really a terror as a child—fantastic temper!"

Cord chuckled at Mary's words. "You forgot to mention Grandmother's temper. I've always thought she cared so much for me because I inherited her temper." In a mockingly tender tone, he added for Stacy's benefit, "Thank heaven, I've learned to control it."

"I'm afraid, Cord, there've been a few times when you've caused us to doubt your words," Bill Buchanan smiled with a dubious shake of his head. "Don't get me wrong, Stacy, I'm sure the right woman would be able to deal with him, but I would hate to be on the receiving end of his temper when it does go out of control.''

Embarrassed by the sly matchmaking of the married couple and the recollection of the controlled display he had shown that day on the road, Stacy murmured a vague response. Thankfully, she was interrupted by Maria announcing that dinner was ready.

''You will be joining us, won't you?'' Cord asked. Mary began to make an excuse, but Cord interjected, ''I'm not taking no for an answer. It's too seldom we have social visits and we won't let you go away so soon, will we, Stacy?''

He extended a hand to her which she was unable to refuse without being obvious. Distracted by his touch, Stacy half heard the lighthearted banter and acceptance by the pair. She felt herself being ushered into the dining room behind them, the tall shoulder of the rancher brushing against her. Her muscles tensed as she stifled a desire to pull violently away from him.

She had baited him at first about their earlier quarrel and became a little personal, acting as hostess when she herself was only a guest. Playing the little charade had amused Stacy at first as she had enjoyed seeing the surprised look in Cord's eyes. But now she had the distinct feeling that he was laughing at her. Somehow he had succeeded in turning the tables on her, making her the brunt of the joke. And she wasn't enjoying it at all.

As if he had read her mind, Cord whispered to her as he seated her at the table, ''You should have checked the rules.''

Stacy's brown eyes looked apprehensively into his, but she couldn't find any words to answer him. His expression as he seated himself opposite her at the head of the table was pleasant, but his eyes hardened speculatively as he watched her flushed cheeks turn away to respond to a question from Mary. Twice during the meal Stacy was forced to look away from the probing glance of the aquiline face. The dinner seemed to last so long that she was sure it would never end. She was so tense she felt she was sitting on a lighted powder-keg that would explode at any moment. But when Maria served the coffee and dessert the conversation was still on safe topics. A tide of relief washed over her at the end in sight.

"Hey, come back!" Mary teased, waving a hand in front of Stacy. "Didn't you hear what I said?"

"I'm sorry, Mary, I'm afraid I was daydreaming."

"I was wondering if your accident had changed your plans, about staying?"

"No, not really," Stacy replied, avoiding Cord's interested look. "I'll be staying a couple more weeks before going back."

"I'm afraid our country is a little too hard on her," Cord interposed with a smile. "After all, Mary, we were raised here and are used to it, but Stacy is from the East. I imagine it's a little tame and boring around here."

"That's not true at all," Stacy retorted impatiently.

"It's just that there's no future here for you, isn't that it?" A sarcastic smile played on Cord's mouth.

"Yes—I mean no," stammered Stacy, recognizing that she was under a subtle attack.

"Now, Cord—" Mary began.

"Surely you realize that the newness of the adventure has probably worn off for her," he interrupted. "After all, how many mountains do you have to see before you've seen them all? A lot of people have come West with grand ideas, only to run back when the inconveniences and isolation have become too much for them."

"I don't mind all that," Stacy denied. "I love this country."

"You know, Mary, it takes stamina to carve out a future in this land." Cord was deliberately ignoring Stacy and addressing his remarks to the redhead on his right. His voice was low and vindictive. "Luxuries become vastly important when you're suddenly denied them after having them all your life."

He's comparing me with his mother! Stacy thought indignantly. "You don't know what you're talking about," she said, crumpling her napkin on the table.

"Of course. How stupid of me not to realize that appearances are deceiving," the mocking tone in his voice and a sarcastic curl on his upper lip. "I should have recognized that behind the high-fashion clothes, the expensive sports car and the blooded horse there beats the heart of a country girl, unspoiled by a life that's catered to her whims."

The room was filled with tension as the two glared across the table at each other. Stacy longed to lash out at him, but she knew she would only be playing into his hands. She sensed the discomfort of the other two at the table. Somehow she managed a feeble laugh.

"It seems you have me figured out." A weak smile on her flushed cheeks. "I'm just a simple country girl."

A flicker of admiration crossed the tanned face, replaced quickly by a derisive gleam.

"'Simple' is a particularly appropriate adjective, as it denotes showing little sense," Cord replied. "You showed a remarkable lack of it when you journeyed unescorted out here where you knew no one, and proceeded to live alone in a remote cabin, unprotected from possible molesters, and went out riding alone on a horse you couldn't control to places you didn't know. By a stroke of luck you're not lying dead out there now."

"I don't think that your guests are interested in your opinions of me and my behaviour," Stacy replied, pushing her chair away from the table.

In the living room, Mary caught up with her.

"What's up with you two?" she asked.

"We just don't get along," Stacy answered, her hands clutched tightly together. She glanced nervously over her shoulder into the other room.

"You seemed so friendly when we first came that, to be honest, I'd hoped you two had made a match of it," Mary went on.

"That's impossible!" Stacy exclaimed, disgust and anger in her voice. "We manage to carry on a civil conversation once in a while, but it always seems to end with us at each other's throats. It's useless to even pretend that we can stand each other. He's so cynical and self-centred that he insists everyone kneel at his feet, and he's not finding me so subservient.''

Immediately upon uttering her words, Stacy felt Cord's presence in the room. Defiantly she turned to face the glowering eyes. The tall man with his broad shoulders seemed to fill the room, diminishing everything near him.

"Our guests are leaving." The dark figure finally spoke. "Are you going to the door with them?"

Stacy turned without answering Cord and walked with Mary as she collected her purse and started towards the front door. Stacy's back prickled ominously, aware of the rancher walking directly behind her. Before reaching the front patio, Stacy murmured an apology to the girl beside her, speaking in a low voice.

"I'm sorry you were dragged into the middle of our fight, Mary. I so enjoyed your coming out here."

"Don't you worry about it," Mary admonished. "It happens to the best of us. You just hurry up and get better."

"I second that," Bill added, putting his hand on Stacy's shoulder. "Professionally speaking, get yourself another couple of days' rest and limit your activities. After that you can do as you want."

Looking up at the pleasant face of the doctor, Stacy gave him a timorous smile. Her pleasure at the kindness of her new friends was overshadowed by the dark man who was standing so close to her that her whole being screamed its knowledge. With cheery good-byes, the couple walked down to their car. A little forlornly, Stacy watched as the car disappeared down the winding lane. Resolutely she turned to face Cord and his scornful eyes, only to find him gone. Glancing quickly around, she saw his familiar form striding towards the stables. Puzzled and relieved at the same time, she walked into the house.

CHAPTER SIX

FOR THE past two days, Stacy had taken special pains to avoid Cord Harris. Her success was achieved with the co-operation of the rancher, who apparently did not want her company either. Digging the toe of her boot into the sandy soil, Stacy looked around the grounds hesitantly. The time had come to talk to him and she wasn't looking forward to it at all. She had fully regained her strength and wanted to make arrangements to return to the cabin. The last of her packing had been completed after lunch, which left her with the unpleasant task of finding Cord. The big German Shepherd padded contentedly along at her side as she wandered past the open doorway of the office. A glance inside verified the inner feeling that he wasn't there. With an impatient sigh Stacy continued to the stables.

"He's probably out on the range somewhere," she thought grimly, gazing out beyond the buildings.

At the corrals she noticed a horse and rider rounding one of the barns at a gallop. Not recognizing the man, Stacy waited. Her curiosity was aroused by his haste. Her ears caught the shouting of voices not far from the stables and she turned to see the reason for the commotion, but the buildings blocked her view.

The rider had just reined his horse to a stop by the corral gate and dismounted.

"What's wrong?" she asked the cowboy.

"'Scuse me, ma'am, but I got to call the doctor," the man murmured, starting to hurry past her.

"What happened? Who got hurt?" Stacy cried, a horrifying picture already forming of Cord lying unconscious on the ground.

"That red devil of a stallion slipped out of the stud pen when Chris went in," he answered, hurrying towards the open office door with Stacy right behind him. "The young fool climbed on his horse and tried to rope him. The horse went berserk and attacked him. Luckily the Boss and us was headed in from off the range and saw what happened. Don't know how bad the kid's hurt—can't get near him."

"Diablo!" Stacy gasped, staring at the man reaching for the phone to the office.

"The Boss is mad enough to kill that horse," muttered the cowboy into the phone, not directing the sentence to Stacy.

As she heard the man reach the doctor, Stacy rushed out of the office towards the standing horse. She jumped on the buckskin and turned him towards the distant sound of voices. Her thoughts were barely coherent as she shouted to the Shepherd to follow and kicked the already winded horse into a gallop. She just knew she had to get there.

"Kill Diablo!" The words rang like a death knell in her ears. Confused, she whipped the horse with the reins as he bounded around the buildings and headed towards the mounted figures beyond. As she drew up by the two mounted horsemen, she saw a rider trapped under his fallen horse with her red stallion between him and the two riders. A rope was flying free from Diablo's neck as he eluded the ropes of the other two riders. His neck and withers were white with foam as he continued to lash out with his wicked hooves.

"What the hell are you doing here?" shouted Cord Harris as he sighted Stacy dismounting her horse. His face was contorted in anger as he swung his big bay around to face her. "Get back to the house where you belong!"

"He's my horse!" shouted Stacy, turning away towards the stallion who was lunging, teeth bared, at the other mounted rider.

"You crazy female," roared the rancher, reining his horse over beside her, "can't you see that damn stud is loco?"

It was then that Stacy noticed the bullwhip in the angry man's hand, the end dragging in the dust raised by the bay's dancing hooves. Fire flashed from her eyes as she raised her head to meet his dark eyes.

"What do you propose to do? Whip him into submission?"

"If I have to, yes. That boy over there is hurt!"

"Get out of my way!" Stacy demanded. Pushing his horse away from her, she walked to face the red stallion.

A shrill whistle rang from Diablo as he pawed the ground and shook his flaxen mane at the solitary figure in front of him. Rearing, he flashed his black hooves through the air, his ears snaked back.

"Diablo!" Stacy commanded, attempting to pierce the frenzied mind of the stallion. "Diablo, settle down!"

His ears remained flat against his head as he lashed out with his back feet at the Shepherd worrying him from behind. Stacy could see the fallen horse attempting to rise, only to fall back on its side. As the stallion started to charge at her, she called to him once again, her voice rising in authority. Stacy thought she saw his ears flicker up as he swept towards her. When he was just about on her, she stepped aside and he thundered by. Spinning around, he faced her, tossing his blazed head. Out of the corner of her eye, Stacy saw the two mounted riders moving. One was headed for the injured rider and Cord was coming towards the stallion, the whip rolled on the saddlehorn and a rope flicking the air in readiness.

"Diablo," her voice changed to a caressing whisper, "easy, boy, settle down. It's all right, baby. Come here. Come on!"

But the excitement and the almost forgotten memory of the scar on his neck was too much. The red horse couldn't curb the demon driving him. His delicate head bobbed up and down, the foam flicking off his neck. He recognized the girl in front of him, but he was filled with a new sense of hate and strength. Out of the corner of his eyes he caught the movement of horse and rider coming up behind him and danced around to face them. Stepping forward Stacy called to him. This time he spun swiftly around and raced towards her, his teeth bared and his head low. When Stacy attempted to jump out of his way, the stallion veered into her, jostling her to the ground with his big shoulder.

Breathless but unhurt, she raised herself up to see Cord streaking after the horse. He yelled at the other horseman and both ropes encircled the red sorrel at the same time. Screaming his anger, the horse attempted to charge the furthest rider, only to be brought up short by the rope dallied around Cord's saddlehorn.

"We got him, Boss! We got him!" yelled the other rider triumphantly, as the horse struggled futilely between the two ropes. It only took him a few minutes to realize he couldn't hope to win. Swiftly the two riders led him to the gate of the stud pen from which he had just escaped.

Dusting herself off, Stacy saw the third rider who had been sent to call the doctor kneeling beside the fallen horse and rider. Hurriedly she made her way over to them, arriving the same time as Cord. His expression was grim as he knelt beside the pain-racked form of the young cowboy.

"Take it easy, Chris," Cord instructed. "We'll have you out of there in no time. Doc's on his way."

"My leg's broken," groaned the young rider, gritting his teeth with pain. "Get me out from under this damned horse!"

"Shortly, how bad's that horse's leg?" demanded Cord, directing his words to the dusty figure trying to quiet the downed gelding. The only answer was a negative shake of the head.

Without a word, Cord rose and walked over to his bay horse and extracted his rifle from the scabbard. Stacy stood numbly watching the action, unable to move or react. The loud report of the gun as it silenced the life of the injured horse deafened her. Overcome by shock and horror, she did not see the doctor arrive or the boy being carried away on a stretcher; the only thing she could see was the inert form of the dead horse. The tears glazing her eyes seemed frozen, too. At last her vision was blocked by Cord's dusty, sweaty form. Stiffly she raised her tear-filled eyes to his blurred face.

"Why?" she whispered, forcing the words through the lump in her throat.

"When Chris roped your horse the sorrel charged, knocking them down, breaking Chris's leg and his horse's, too. The doc says he's going to be all right, six weeks or so off the leg and on crutches for a month or more."

"No," Stacy mumbled, barely coherent. "The horse! Why did you have to kill him? It wasn't his fault," she sobbed. It was her first experience with what seemed to her brutality and she couldn't keep her eyes from straying to the dead horse.

"The horse?" exploded Cord. "Do you realize that I could have lost a man? A human being! And all you're worried about is a horse!"

His anger pierced her shock and she turned to his face again and read the distaste and disgust that filled it. He didn't understand. She was upset about the rider, but she couldn't reconcile herself to the cold-blooded killing of the horse.

"But he's going to be all right, don't you understand? He'll be back, but the horse is dead and you killed him! As if it was nothing!'' Her voice was shrill with shock and near-hysteria.

"Nothing? Do you realize that I'm now without a horse and a rider? Do you think it's going to be easy to replace a man at this time of the year?'' he roared, grabbing her arm in a vicelike grip. "I have you to thank for that, you and that horse of yours!''

"Oh, sure, it's all my fault,'' she cried sarcastically. "Well, don't worry. I'll pay for the hospital bills and any inconvenience this caused you.''

"You're damned right you will!'' Cord replied. His voice lowered threateningly. "But your money won't buy your way out of this one. You're going to take Chris's place. For once in your life, you're going to see what it's like to work to pay a debt.''

"What are you talking about?'' Stacy asked, her body now trembling with anger.

"You've gained a lot of sympathy with that poor orphan act of yours around here. I bet it really broke your heart when your father died and left you all that money,'' he replied, scorn and contempt deep in his voice.

His words cut like a knife into her heart as the horrible accusation left Stacy speechless. Unconsciously she felt the contact of her hand against his cheek. Her palm was stinging as the deepening fire in his eyes once again focused on her.

"So that's the way the little cat plays,'' he murmured through clenched teeth. "Today you got away with it, but I wouldn't try it again if I were you. You start to work tomorrow,'' he stated. "And wear

something practical, like jeans. We don't hold any
fashion shows out on the range.''

Her feet were rooted to the ground and the angry
tears in her eyes trickled down her cheeks as she
watched Cord stalk away. Her hands were clenched
into tight fists as she tried to find the words to scream
after him. But her mouth refused to open and the
words never came out. She stood there shaking with
uncontrolled anger that gradually gave way to gasp-
ing sobs. Cord Harris had already mounted his horse
and ridden off in the direction of the ranch house before Stacy moved from her position. Slowly she made
her way in the same direction, her mind jumbled with
thoughts of hatred for the rancher and compassion for
the injured boy and the dead horse.

By the time Stacy reached the yards, the dust from
the ranch car was halfway down the road. Silently she
made her way to the hacienda, oblivious to her actual
surroundings. Once inside the house and in her bedroom, Stacy sat on the bed and looked at the posses-
sions she had earlier collected to leave.

With one hand she wiped the angry tears away from
her eyes as she sat going over again their conversation. It was wrong to be concerned for the horse as
opposed to a human being, but it had been the shock
of the horse's death. Perhaps she was even wrong to
accuse Cord of brutally killing the horse without a
thought if he could be saved or not. But Stacy could
find no excuse for his outrageous attack against her
about her father's death. Besides, she had never told
him that she was orphaned, though she had told the
Nolans, but no one, certainly, knew about the money

she had inherited! The anger in her heart faded away and was replaced by the crushing feeling of despair. How could she ever hope to convince him that this wasn't true! But why should she try? The confusion of her thoughts drove her to her feet and she paced the room. Resentment of Cord Harris boiled inside her.

Just exactly how was he going to make her stay against her will? He certainly couldn't force her to work. And besides, just exactly what did she know about ranching? Stacy stopped in front of the mirror, an idea forming in her mind. He couldn't stop her leaving because he wasn't even here. She glanced quickly at her watch and just as quickly outside. More time had gone by than she realized. The sun was already down and Cord must have been gone for at least two hours. If she intended to leave before he returned, she didn't have much time. Quickly she began gathering her belongings and setting them outside her room.

Naturally, he would accuse her of running away and refusing to face his challenge, but let him think what he liked. Unfortunately she had been forced to accept his hospitality when she was ill, but there was no need to stay any longer. It was enough that she had offered to pay the hospital bill for the boy and reimburse Cord for the horse. If financially she was unable to pay him, that would be the time to try to arrange some way to work the problem out. Even she had to admit that she was responsible for her horse.

Stacy had just slipped her fringed jacket on and picked up her purse and started out of the bedroom when she heard the big oak door close. Numbly she stood beside her luggage and stared at the tall form standing at the bottom of the stairs. Cord's features were hidden in the shadows, but Stacy could well imagine the dark brows gathered together and the clean, hard set of his jaw, and most of all the grim line of his mouth. Her eyes were wide and darkening with apprehension as she felt the trembling course through her body. Neither spoke as the tension grew.

"I take it you're planning on going somewhere?" came the low baritone voice.

"What if I do?" Stacy retorted defiantly, lifting her chin in challenge.

"Then I would suggest you forget it," was the cool reply as Cord stepped out of the shadows. There were new lines on his face that Stacy hadn't noticed before, but there was no mistaking the hard quality in his voice. He cast one further glance at the luggage and the still figure above him. "You might as well unpack."

"You don't actually believe you can keep me a prisoner here against my will?" Stacy exploded, in anger.

He gave her one brief glance before replying. "You're in my debt and it's up to me to set the terms of payment."

The hopelessness of fighting this man raced through Stacy and her shoulders slumped slightly, acknowledging defeat. The fire went out in her eyes and was replaced with despair and confusion. Struggling, she attempted to take one last stand. "I will not stay in that room one more night!"

A glint of amusement showed in his eyes before he turned his face away from her.

"As you like. There's a guestroom down the hall. Use it," he paused briefly. "In case you're interested, the boy's going to be in the hospital for a few weeks and inactive for a couple of months."

Stacy felt the heat rising in her cheeks at her inconsideration for not asking about the injured rider's condition. Why did he always manage to make her seem so heartless? Frustrated, she gathered up her case and stalked into the hallway, stopping at the first doorway on her left.

She was too upset to take in the surroundings of the room. Her anger was too close to the surface to allow her to dwell on anything but Cord's dark eyes and sculptured face. His cool indifference irritated her. All she had done was make a fool of herself and increase his belief that she was spoiled and selfish. Stacy knew she could expect no mercy at his hands. He expected her to take the rider's place regardless of her sex.

"Very well, Mr. Harris," she whispered to herself. "I can take anything you can dish out. No quarter asked."

THE SUN had barely touched the sky the following morning when there was a loud knock at Stacy's door. Sleepily she raised herself up on one elbow and looked out the window and then over to the clock on the dresser. It took her a minute before she remembered the previous day's events.

"Yes?"

"It's time to get up," came Cord's voice from the hall. "That is if you want coffee and some breakfast before work."

He didn't wait for a reply, but strode away from the door. Determinedly, Stacy clambered out of the bed. It took her only a few minutes to dress in her Levi's and shirt and to tie her hair back at the nape of her neck. A little smile played on her soft lips as she looked at the image reflected in the mirror. If Mr. Harris thought that blue jeans and a plain blouse were going to make her look less of a woman then he was wrong. She couldn't keep the pleasure out of her eyes as she surveyed her gentle curves. She checked to make sure her riding gloves were in the pocket of her suede jacket, picked up her hat and walked down the stairs to the dining room.

Unfortunately Cord wasn't there. Stacy queried Maria, who replied that Mr. Harris had already taken his meal and was out giving instructions to the men. Maria was plainly confused by the turn of events and kept casting puzzled glances at the young girl. When Stacy finished her toast and coffee, Maria said that Stacy was to meet the Boss out in the yard.

Gratefully Stacy realized that most of the men had already gone. It would have been embarrassing to be subjected to the forbidding rancher's orders in the presence of his men. As it was, she recognized his tall form still talking to two men. His back was to her, so he didn't see her approach, but Stacy was sure he knew she was coming.

The two men standing with him attempted to ignore the approaching girl. The taller of the two was only a few years older than Stacy and obviously embarrassed by the situation. He kept his head down, his hat preventing Stacy from seeing the expression on his face. The other man was considerably older and wizened. The constant sun on his face had made his skin so leathery that Stacy was unable to judge his age. When she approached the group the older one met her gaze openly, compassion and sympathy etched in the eyes that squinted in the morning sun. It was a comfort to recognize an ally here.

"It's about time you got here, Adams," Cord said crisply, turning his aquiline features towards her. "I want you to go with Hank and Jim today to gather the stock cattle in the winter range," he ordered, casting only a cursory glance at the petite figure beside him. "Any other questions, Hank?"

The older man shook his head negatively.

"Okay, mount up."

Stacy started to follow the two men as they walked to the horses standing saddled on the other side of the corral, but was called back by Cord. Turning to face the imposing figure, she took her gloves out of her jacket pocket and began putting them on her hands, hoping to stave off the nervousness she felt facing him.

"Yes," she said, looking boldly into his face, her voice matching the crisp tone he had used earlier. She was unable to read his dark expression.

For a minute he didn't answer, then he said, "Hank will show you all that needs to be done."

"All right," she replied, disliking the searching eyes that seemed to probe deep inside her. "Anything else?"

"No. Good luck." His tone was indifferent and conflicting with his words.

Briskly Stacy turned from him and walked to where the two mounted riders waited. The one named Hank handed her the reins of a short-coupled bay pony. Silently she mounted and turned her horse to follow the other two.

Shortly after leaving the ranchyard, the younger of the two men rode ahead, leaving the wizened old cowboy alone with Stacy. Normally she would have been enjoying the early morning ride, but today's circumstances made her conscious of the humiliating position she was in. Pride forbade her to look at the silent, hunched figure beside her. For a time the two horses moved along at their slow, shuffling trot, until the rider beside her pulled his horse into a walk and Stacy's mount automatically matched the pace.

"Miss Adams," came the questioning, rough voice, "now it ain't none of my business and you can tell me to shut my mouth, but if we're going to be riding the range together, it gets mighty lonely if all you can talk to is yore hoss. Now, it ain't in me to question the Boss's orders, but me nor none of the boys hold you responsible for what happened to the kid the other day. It's gonna be a long day in the saddle, specially for a dude like you, but it shore does make the day go faster if there's a bit of jawin' goin' on."

Stacy had the distinct impression that this was the longest statement the man had ever made, and she smiled at his thoughtfulness. He was trying to put her at ease in his own clumsy way and himself as well.

"Thank you, Hank. I appreciate it more than you know."

"Well, I been working on this spread ever since the Boss was in knee-britches, and I seen some strange things. But I gotta admit this is the first time we've ever had us a lady wrangler. An' the Boss says you gotta pull your own weight," he said, shaking his head in confusion.

"I intend to, too," Stacy replied, a grim look of determination on her face. "I don't know anything about ranching or cows, but I can learn. At least I can ride and am in fair shape."

"Well, now, miss, I reckon you can ride all right, but you gotta relax a little more. Ya ain't in no hoss show, so you don't have to worry 'bout how you look," Hank said with a slight smile. "An' I'd watch what you call cows. Safe thing is to call 'em cattle."

"I stand corrected," she laughed. "Tell me, Hank, what exactly are we doing today?"

"We're gonna be rattlin' the brush for bunch-quitters mostly an' gettin' the herd ready for movin' to the summer pasture. Most of the men trucked their horses to the far end of the pasture an'll be workin' towards us with the main herd."

"Trucked their horses?" Stacy asked quizzically, her brown eyes examining the weathered face of the cowboy.

"Yep. It's a modern West you'll find. Rather than spendin' a lot of time ridin' to where the herd is, now they jus' load the horses up in trucks or trailers and haul 'em as close as they can."

"It's a miracle they don't use Jeeps to round them up," Stacy exclaimed half to herself, in amazement.

"A few years ago when we was really tryin' to gather all the scrub bulls an' strays, the Boss ordered a helicopter to search 'em out. Things have changed," Hank muttered. "Reckon we ought to catch up with Jim?"

The brisk morning air was beginning to warm with the rising sun. Already the morning dew was rapidly vanishing from the undergrowth wherever the sun's rays probed through the shade. The distant mountainous hills were cloaked in a golden haze that cast its shimmering glow upon the grassland stretched out below it. The morning air was bereft of any breeze and the stillness was broken only by the shuffling trot of the three cow-ponies and the occasional call of the quail. The three riders travelled several miles before arriving at the first barbed wire fence. They rode along the fence until they arrived at a gate. Stacy and Hank waited astride their horses while Jim manoeuvred his horse into position to unhook the gate and open it for the other two. After they had passed through, the young cowboy followed, closing the gate behind him.

"This is where we start to work, miss," the wizened cowboy said, indicating the land spread out before them.

"But I don't see any cattle," said Stacy, looking at the vacant pasture.

"That's the general idea. If they was right out in plain sight it wouldn't be quite so much work. But they seem to know every ravine and bush on the spread and that's where they plan to stay."

"But I thought that you raised domestic cattle, a Hereford cross of some sort?" she queried, plainly puzzled.

"We do, but they been left alone. They're just about as skittish of humans as the old longhorns that used to graze this land. Only difference between the two is these ain't half as ornery as them," Hank replied squinting his eyes to look over the land. "We usually split up a bit here, but you stick close to me for a while, miss."

The three riders loped off; the younger cowboy moved fifty yards to their left and they all began scouring the brush. It was hot dusty work for horse and rider, and it wasn't long before Stacy removed her jacket and tied it on the back of the saddle. Between the heat of the sun and the constant exercise, Stacy's bay began perspiring, too. They scared up a couple of head of cattle, as they worked their way along. Stacy began to respect the game horse she was riding. By mid-morning they had about fifteen head of cattle driving in front of them. Hank instructed the young girl to keep them going while he and Jim added other strays with them.

At first she thought he was giving her an easier job until she began breathing in the dust that the cattle were kicking up. She wasn't even able to relax on the horse. Every time she allowed her attention to wander from the herd that was the precise time that one of the animals decided to make another break for the open bush. The little bay instinctively gave chase and cut it back into the herd. Quite a few times Stacy was positive that the horse was going to spin around and send her flying in the other direction. Her legs were so weary from gripping his sides and her body so covered with dust and grime and sweat that she was sure that she wouldn't make it through the rest of the morning let alone the whole day. Each time one of the cowboys added another steer to the herd, Stacy could hardly stop from sighing outwardly. She had learned for every steer in the herd her horse had to cover twice their distance.

Her mouth was dry and gritty, but she was afraid to sip out of her canteen for fear that one of the herd would decide to leave. The girl was happy to see Hank ride up alongside, but trying to smile a hello was an effort. He didn't look at her directly, but Stacy could still recognize a ghost of a smile on his face.

"Mighty dirty work, ridin' drag on a bunch of scrubs,'" he murmured in the air. "We're comin' up on the water tank where we'll meet up with the chuck wagon for lunch. Reckon maybe you could do with a rest, huh?"

"I don't mind admitting that I could, Hank," Stacy replied, feeling her lips crack as she spoke. Giving the little bay an affectionate pat on the neck, she added, "I think he deserves one too."

"The remuda will be there. His work is done for the day," the cowboy answered.

"Oh, look!" cried Stacy, turning her attention to the left. "Isn't that Jim coming?—and it looks like he's got a little baby calf across his saddle."

The younger cowboy joined them with a new white-faced calf lying crosswise on his saddle with the mother following alongside, lowing soothingly to her youngster.

"He's darling!" Stacy exclaimed. "How old is he?"

"Just a couple of days," Jim replied, the shyness still evident in his failure to look directly at Stacy, but proud of her interest in his find. "I found them out in the brush. The calf wasn't able to keep up, so I thought I'd give him a ride to the calf wagon."

"Calf wagon? What's that?" Stacy asked, her attention diverted from the snow-white face.

"There's usually a bunch of these latecomers that are too little to keep up with the herd, so we have a trailer we put 'em in until we reach the night's holdin' ground and then we mammy 'em up," Hank replied, amused at Stacy's concern for the calf. "Take the little critter on in, Jim, we'll be there shortly."

"Isn't that what you call a dogey, a baby calf?" Stacy asked watching as Jim rode on ahead.

"A dogey is really a calf without a momma, but a lot o' people call all calves dogies," Hank answered.

"The cattle have settled down a lot. It must be your being here. Before, every five minutes one was heading in a different direction," Stacy commented, enjoying the conversation with the knowledgeable cowboy.

"Nope, it's not me. They smell water. We just happen to be going the same direction as them."

The cattle and two riders topped a small rise in the ground and came upon a high plateau covered with tall stands of pampas grass and creosote bushes. Ahead Stacy could see the large water tank and windmill. Beyond that was a station wagon and several pick-ups and trailers. A look of astonishment crossed her dust-stained face.

"That's the chuck wagon?"

A dry chuckle escaped the old cowboy's throat. "I told ya the old West was gone. They bring the food from the ranch house and trailer the remuda to the noon stop," the old man smiled. "You go on and ride ahead. These cattle ain't goin' nowhere 'cept to that tank. Rest while you can. We're gonna be hittin' the saddle for another long afternoon."

Gratefully, Stacy reined her little bay out around the herd and set him at a lope for the waiting vehicles. She rode over to where a cowboy waited by the trailers. There were already several riders over by the station wagon; some were eating and some were just getting their food. Behind the trailers Stacy noticed a couple of Mexicans cooling off some cow-ponies with replacements picketed along the trailers. Slowly she dismounted. Her bones and muscles were so sore that she stood for a minute to adjust to the solid ground beneath her feet. Now that she was on the ground, she wasn't so sure that she could walk. She took a few careful steps in the general direction of the wagon and realized that she was going to navigate all right under her own power, so she joined the men at the station wagon where they were dishing out food from the rear.

The good-natured grumbling and banter that had been going on when Stacy rode up had stopped, and Stacy became uneasy. She had been so comfortable with the old cowboy, and so tired and hungry from the skimpy breakfast, that she neglected to remember her awkward position. With a red face and a trembling hand she accepted the dish of stew and beans with a thick slice of bread alongside from one of the cooks and a steaming mug of coffee from another. Nervously she turned around to search for a shaded place to have her meal. All eyes were on her as she turned; some looked away abruptly while others eyed her boldly.

"Ma'am," came a hesitant voice from her right. Stacy turned and with relief recognized the young rider, Jim. "If you like, you can join me. Not many shaded places left."

"Thank you, Jim," she said, looking for the first time into the hazel eyes of the young cowboy. "I guess I did look a little lost."

"Yes, you mustn't mind the men. They aren't used to seeing women around camp," he replied, removing his hat to run his fingers through his bleached brown hair. There was a boyishness about his face that deceived his true age which was in the middle twenties.

In between bites of food, Stacy asked, "Have you worked here long?"

"Off and on all my life. Got out of the service a couple years ago and went to college, but I work here in the summers for tuition money," he replied, a look of seriousness crossing his face.

"What are you studying?"

"Forestry, conservation," was the quiet answer.

"Are you planning to be a park ranger?" Stacy inquired.

"Hopefully. Mr. Harris has suggested coming back to the ranch, but I think I'd rather not. Initially I was going to be a vet., but I discovered that I was more interested in the agricultural and ecological side,'' he answered, enjoying the interest Stacy was taking in him.

"I wouldn't let Mr. Harris's wishes interfere with what I wanted to do," Stacy said, a trace of bitterness in her voice as she stabbed at a piece of beef in the stew.

"No, of course not," came the low, mocking reply.

Stacy jerked her head up and practically choked on the piece of meat as she stared into the tanned face of the rancher. Jim scrambled to his feet in embarrassment.

"We were just discussing my college plans, sir," he stated, his jaw clenched tight, defending Stacy in his own way from the sardonic smile of his employer.

Swiftly Stacy got to her feet to prevent any further remarks on her behalf. It was humiliating enough to have to look up to Cord, but to be seated at his feet was too much. Cord Harris shifted his gaze from the young cowhand to the hatless girl before him. Boldly she met his gaze, conscious once again of her dust-covered clothes and face.

"Perhaps you would like to go check on your horses for Miss Adams, Connors," Cord suggested with a definite tone of dismissal.

The cowboy cast a wavering glance at the girl at his side. Stacy smiled at him with a great deal more confidence than she felt. Her pulse was racing at an unsettling pace. Reluctantly Jim Connors left the two standing alone beside the trailer.

"You seem to have gained yourself an admirer."

"Don't be ridiculous! He was only being polite. He obviously has been taught some manners—which is more than I can say for some people," Stacy said scathingly.

"I see you've managed to survive the morning in fair shape." Cord ignored her insult and leaned against the side of the trailer to light a cigarette. Unconsciously he held the match until it was cool, all the while his gaze travelling over the dirty face of the girl.

"Yes. I managed quite well. Surprised?"

"No. I imagine you could do anything you set your mind to," he replied. "I only wonder if you have the staying power."

"Hey, Boss, is that the filly you picked up at the sale last week?" Hank walked up beside them, his attention fixed on a chestnut sorrel at the far end of the trailer. The horse didn't like being tied up and pawed the ground impatiently while pulling at the reins. "Shore is a nice-looking thing."

Cord's eyes never left Stacy's face. "Yes, she is."

Stacy could feel herself begin to blush, but she couldn't break away from the compelling eyes.

"Do ya think she's gonna be able to settle down to ranch life?" Hank asked, and then addressed his next remark to Stacy, not noticing that she was paying little attention to him. "She was raced a few times and she's used to a lot of fuss and bother. Spoilt, you might say."

A mocking smile crossed Cord's lips as he watched the discomfiture registering on Stacy's face. "It's hard to tell, Hank."

"Shore seems awful fractious. It'll take a lot of patience to change this one's way of thinkin'," the old cowboy went on with a shake of his head.

"It will that," Cord said with a throaty laugh. "It will that. Well, mustn't detain you two any longer from your work. I'll see you later."

With no more than a brief nod to Stacy and a friendly slap on the back to the cowhand, Cord strode over to where the young horse stood tethered, the secretly amused expression still on his face. Untying the reins, he swung his tall frame easily into the saddle as the spirited horse danced beneath him. He didn't even glance in their direction as he reined the sorrel over towards a group of riders talking over their last cup of coffee. Stacy couldn't hear what was said, but gathered it was an order to mount up, because shortly after they dispersed and walked over to where their ponies were tied.

Out of the corner of her eye, she saw Jim walking up leading two horses. He handed her the reins to a big Roman-nosed buckskin. Stacy could tell that Jim was embarrassed about leaving her in Cord's clutches, but at this moment the tanned face was still plainly visible in her mind and the delicious, throaty laugh was still echoing in her ears. Silently they mounted and rode over to join the grizzled cowhand, Hank, and get at the afternoon's work.

CHAPTER SEVEN

STACY HAD thought the morning long and arduous, but by six o'clock that evening she knew the true meaning of bone-weary. She yearned to give a cry of joy when she sighted the windmill that indicated the night's holding ground for the cattle.

Her failure to try to shirk her work off on to them had gained her both Jim and Hank's respect. Several times they would have taken over for her, but she hadn't let them. It would have been easy for her to trade on her womanhood, and they would have allowed it, in spite of their employer's order.

Hank suggested that she ride on ahead and get a cup of coffee for each of them, but she declined, saying with a tired attempt at a laugh that she was going to need help getting off her horse. At the moment it seemed almost too true to be funny. A short time later they hazed their small herd in with the main one settling down for the night about a hundred yards from the camp.

A sense of peace cloaked the riders as they rode back into the strange western camp of motorized vehicles where the odour of petrol and oil mixed with the smell of sweaty horses, cattle, and humans. Good-naturedly Stacy accepted the helping hand of the younger cowboy as she dismounted. She felt no self-consciousness as she limped her way to the station wagon and the promising aroma of coffee. Hank had arrived before the other two and was talking to the riders who had gathered around the lowered tailgate.

"Hank," Stacy groaned, looking into the grey eyes, a smile of mock pain on her face, "I think you're looking at the very first bow-legged lady wrangler. I'll never walk straight again as long as I live, let alone be able to sit down!"

There was a considerable amount of sympathizing laughter from the group and, more important, acceptance. Accompanied by a goodly amount of jesting and joking, Stacy was presented with a steaming cup of the cook's java. After inhaling the steam rising from the cup, she emitted an audible sigh of appreciation.

"Cook, you are a master chef, but tell me, where is the bath water?" she exclaimed, and met with another round of laughter. "Do you boys go through this every day?"

"Twice on Sunday," one of them replied, and laughed at the expression of mock disbelief on Stacy's face.

"Spare me the details and help me find a way to sit down!"

Several of the riders stepped forward, including Jim Connors, and with exaggerated care lowered her to the ground. Despite her aches and pains, Stacy was beginning to enjoy herself, and so were the men. There had seldom been a woman in their midst and definitely none that had joined in making fun of herself and her situation. With a sparkle in her eyes, she started to make another comment to the men, only to notice that they had grown very quiet and were looking beyond her. Still in a jovial mood, she turned her radiant smile to include the object of their attention. Cord Harris's frame had cast its shadow over the group. His expression was a study of amused interest in the girl and the surrounding riders. Stacy couldn't say why or how she had the nerve to say what came next.

"Oh, Patrón, please allow this lowly peon to remain seated in thy great presence, for I vow I couldn't rise if you commanded me."

There was a chilling stillness as the men waited for their boss to answer. Stacy was horrified at her words, but it was too late to retract them. She held her breath along with the men. The low chuckle that finally came relaxed everyone and most of all the seated Stacy.

"Charlie, give me a cup of that brew of yours while I sit down beside this señorita," Cord directed with a grin to the cook.

Someone had started a campfire, and Stacy fixed her attention on it rather than the disconcerting man beside her, trying to ignore the delicious chill that had quaked her body at his pleasant laugh. The sun was beginning to set now, casting its coloured shadows on the countryside, while the two sipped their coffee in silence. The cook brought them a plate of beefsteak and beans and refilled their coffee.

"Well, what do you think of the cattle drive?" Cord asked as they began eating their meal. "Is it what you expected it to be?"

"No," Stacy replied with a smile, "not meant as a complaint, but it's a lot harder work than I thought."

"So far you've come through with flying colours," he said.

"Meaning you don't think I'll last."

"Meaning I have no opinion except that you've done very well." There was a mocking glint in his eyes as he went on, "You really should do something about that temper of yours. You're a little too quick to take offence."

"Perhaps I've had cause," Stacy replied, her gaze still occupied by the flickering campfire flames.

"Touché," Cord smiled, his eyes observing the still face. "I imagine you're pretty tired after today's work. The remuda hands will be heading back to the ranch house shortly. You can catch a ride with them, or wait a little longer and I'll give you a ride back."

"Is everyone going back?" Stacy was astounded. "You mean you just leave the cattle unattended to stray all over?"

"No," Cord chuckled, "most of the men will be staying and taking their turns at riding herd. They've brought along their bedrolls," he added, indicating places where some of the men had already made them up.

"Then why am I going back to the ranch?"

"Because you didn't come prepared for staying overnight and because it wouldn't be permissible for a woman to spend the night out here on a trail drive," Cord replied a little curtly. "Plus you've only been out of a sickbed a few days. It would be foolish to overdo it."

"Oh, but I'm just one of the boys, remember?" Stacy mocked, her brown eyes flashing bright sparks, magnified by the burning embers.

"During the day," he qualified in his crisp tone.

"I'm staying the night here." Stacy's voice was low and determined.

"You will be returning with me."

"Then you'll have to carry me forcibly from here and that would make quite a scene. But then you don't mind scenes, do you?"

"You're forgetting that you have no place to sleep," Cord stated. "Didn't you learn from your last experience what can happen staying out in the cold at night?"

"I'm quite sure I'll be able to make some sort of arrangement to borrow a blanket or something from someone."

"Or perhaps share a bedroll?" was the sarcastic reply. "I'm sure you'd have plenty of offers."

"You dirty-minded beast!" Stacy exclaimed, forgetting the tired muscles in her body and bounding to her feet. The fury mounted in her face as she waited for Cord to join her. "I don't know what kind of women you're familiar with, but let me assure you that I don't fit in that category!" Her voice rose as she struggled to keep control of herself. "I don't have to listen to that kind of talk from any man!"

Cord grabbed hold of her arm, preventing her from running away from him. Trembling, Stacy stopped, neither attempting to pull away from his vicelike grip nor turning to face his cold dark eyes.

"Are you hoping one of your knights will come to your rescue?" he asked in a mocking whisper that she just barely heard.

Unable to reply, she stood immobile. Finally she heard a sigh leave his lips at the same time as he released her arm.

"I believe an apology is in order. Therefore I apologize for the insinuations made and will make accommodation for you to spend the night here," Cord said quietly.

Still Stacy did not turn to face him. There were hot tears of humiliation and hurt in her eyes as she felt his hands touch her shoulders and slowly turn her around to face him. With surprising gentleness his large hand cupped her chin and raised it up so that he could see her face. His own expression was hidden by the shadow of his Stetson hat.

"I guess we're both a little tired and on edge," came the familiar deep voice. "Get a good night's rest."

Cord turned quietly and left. She was conscious of a feeling of emptiness as the chill of night stole over her shoulders and face where a moment ago his hands had been. The anger had vanished, leaving Stacy staring off into the dark after him. Uncertain, she turned back to the flickering campfire and the quiet figures of the ranch hands.

Jim Connors walked up to her from behind one of the trailers carrying a bedroll and a blanket. His bright, questioning hazel eyes searched her face, but Stacy accepted the bedding with only a quiet thank-you and walked over to the other side of the fire. Dully she watched some of the hands loading horses into vans and start pulling out. Involuntarily she searched the darkened forms for Cord and strained to catch the quiet conversation for the sound of his voice, but with no success.

She slipped under the covers of her bedroll and stared up into the dark blue sky overhead, plagued by a variety of emotions—hurt, anger, humiliation, resentment, but most of all a wonder and mystification towards this unpredictable Cord Harris. At last the tired muscles claimed her attention and ignorant of the hard ground and chilling air she drifted off to sleep.

SHE WAS sure she had just barely fallen asleep when a hand began gently shaking her shoulder. Her eyes fluttered open to a starlit sky. Stacy had difficulty focusing on the figure beside her in the absence of light. At first she thought it was Cord, but then she recognized the smaller build of Jim Connors.

"It's time to get up."

"It's dark yet," she muttered, sleep heavy in her voice.

"It's four o'clock," the young cowboy answered lightly. "We rise early around here. Breakfast is almost ready. Better get washed up."

A moment later he was gone. Painfully Stacy rolled out of her bed, all of her muscles crying out for her not to move. It was all she could do to stand up. Stiffly she walked over to a basin of water warmed by the rekindled fire. Gratefully she splashed the water on her face, enjoying the clean sensation it gave her skin. Awake now, she glanced around the camp with interest.

Everywhere there was activity. Horses and riders were walking along the outside of the camp and other riders were mumbling sleepily over their coffee and flapjacks. Over to the east, the sky was beginning to lighten with the coming dawn.

While she was eating the enormous breakfast Jim had brought her, Stacy saw the remuda trucks approaching with a load of fresh horses for the day's work. Since Jim had already finished his breakfast he offered to get her a mount for the morning. A few minutes later he returned leading a big, rangy sorrel and a smaller-built pinto. Quickly Stacy finished off the last of her pancakes and carried the plate and mug over to the station wagon. Several of the riders had already left when she returned to the waiting cowboy. Hank had joined him, mounted on his horse.

"Ready for another day, miss?" he asked, a smile spreading over his tanned face. Watching her slip her hat on, he added, "Now a real cowboy puts his hat on as soon as he gets up."

"I'm still learning," she laughed in return, taking the pinto's reins from Jim. "What's the agenda this morning?"

"Gotta sweep the east side of the main herd for strays," he replied, swinging his pony in that direction.

A groan passed Stacy's lips as she mounted her horse. It was a mixture of dismay at the orders and a rebellion of her sore muscles at returning to the saddle.

"Is Mr. Harris joining the drive today?" she asked.

"Oh, he stayed the night last night and took one of the watches," replied the older cowboy. "Imagine he's headin' the herd up now."

"Oh," Stacy murmured. The idea that Cord had spent the night in the camp was oddly disquieting to her.

"It's a gorgeous morning," she exclaimed as her pony danced beside Jim's mount as if in emphasis of her words. The sun was climbing the sky now, chasing away the last vestiges of the night's shadows.

"It's spring," the young cowboy replied, capturing the exuberance of the attractive girl at his side.

"And it's a beautiful country to be in, in spring!" she laughed. "It makes you feel great just to be alive!"

"You really like it here—in Texas, I mean?"

"I love it," Stacy answered, not noting his qualifying words. "There's room here. I mean, you feel free. No one's crowding you. It's hard to describe."

"I know," Jim replied, his eyes studying her face. "Let's ride over this way. I'd like to show you something."

"What is it?"

"You'll see," he said, looking ahead as they altered their course to the left. "What brought you here to Texas?"

For a minute Stacy didn't answer, but there was something about the young man with his close-cropped brown hair that made her want to confide in him.

"My father was killed in a plane crash about a month and a half ago," she answered quietly. "We were very close. You see, my mother died a few months after I was born, so all there ever was was my father and me."

Jim studied the girl quietly with his hazel eyes, but didn't interrupt her.

"He was a freelance photographer, quite famous in his field. From almost the time I could walk he took me with him on his assignments. I was never in one place long enough to make any real friends. Oh, there were a few that you always got reacquainted with when you returned somewhere," Stacy added, her thoughts turning to Carter Mills, "but it really all boiled down to each other. Dad had chartered a plane to fly us back to Washington after a trip into Tennessee. Over the mountains we developed engine trouble and crashed."

There was a silence for a time while Stacy fought to control the lump in her throat. Staring in front of her, she began to speak again. "Cajun, my German Shepherd, was along. I was knocked unconscious, but somehow he managed to pull me out of the plane and shortly afterwards it burst into flames. My father was still inside."

"Your father was Joshua Adams," said Jim.

"Yes," she answered, a whispered hoarseness creeping into her voice. "Afterwards I was confused. A lot of Dad's friends and colleagues offered to help, but I didn't really know what they could do." A stilted laugh came from her lips. "He always loved the West. I guess I came out here for two reasons, to be close to him and to find what I wanted out of life."

"You've been here before?"

"Not here specifically, but Dad had assignments in El Paso several times and various other places in Arizona and New Mexico," Stacy answered, then added with a laugh, "I really didn't expect to spend my time chasing cattle!"

Understanding that she was trying to shake off the sadness that talking about her father had raised, Jim Connors joined in with her laugh.

"No, I don't imagine you did. Hank and I were along with the Boss when he found you that morning on the range."

"You were?"

"The Boss was fit to be tied when he found your horse," Jim stated, smiling over at the girl. "He was the first one to spot your dog and reach you. None of us had ever seen him in such a state before. He was snapping orders around so fast and wouldn't let anyone else near you but him."

"He was probably afraid I'd sue him for allowing that snake to be on his property," Stacy laughed, ignoring the inquisitive glance.

"You two don't get along very well," Jim commented.

"It's not my fault. I think he just hates women in general," she replied.

"No, I don't believe that," the cowboy said with a dubious shake of his head. "After his engagement to Lydia, I don't believe he's taken women at face value any more. He's forgotten the word trust."

"Whatever his problem is, it's not mine."

"The place I wanted to show you is right over here," Jim said, turning his pony abruptly to the right towards a small hill. "I was in a lecture class where your father was a guest speaker. I think you'll appreciate this."

The two riders topped a small rise to view a meadow covered with a sea of blue flowers. They paused briefly on the hill as Stacy gazed awestruck at the beauty of the multiple blossoms waving brightly in the morning breeze. Mother Nature had covered the hill in a luxurious blanket of deep blue. In the distance they could hear the songs of birds bringing the earth alive on that hill.

"It's beautiful, Jim. What are they?" Stacy exclaimed at last.

"Bluebonnets."

"Such a beautiful blue, almost purple." Her gaze remained on the flowers. "They put the sky to shame."

"Shall we ride down?" he asked.

Stacy didn't answer, but touched the pinto's flank with her heel. Single file the pair rode down the hill to the meadow, stopping in the midst of the indigo profusion. Jim dismounted before Stacy and helped her off her pony. His hand remained on her elbow as they walked companionably amongst the flowers. Stacy couldn't resist picking a small bouquet and inhaling the sweet fragrance.

"I'm so glad you brought me here," Stacy said, turning to face the young cowboy. She only had to raise her eyes a few inches to look into the light hazel ones.

The hand that had been on her elbow slipped up to her shoulder, and the cowboy's other hand moved to rest on the opposite side. The bouquet held in Stacy's hands was the only thing separating them when they both heard the sound of an approaching horse. Simultaneously they turned to face the hoofbeats. It only took Stacy an instant to recognize the rider sitting so straight in the saddle and the blood began pounding in her heart. Cord Harris reined his horse down the hill towards the couple, stopping just short of them.

"Am I interrupting something?" came the implying tone. Not giving either one a chance to answer, he rested an arm on the saddlehorn and said, "Then let's get back to work and save the flowers for off-duty hours."

Both Stacy and Jim mounted their ground-hitched horses with a certain amount of chagrin, fully conscious of the accusing dark eyes. Once on their way again, the rancher nudged his horse between the pair as if separating two naughty children. Stacy's lips set in a grim line, resentful of the childish way Cord was treating them. He was unmindful of her displeasure. After they had left the meadow of bluebonnets, Cord turned his head slightly towards the quiet cowboy riding on his left.

"I want you to ride back to the main herd and help Jenkins on the point, Connors. I'll accompany Miss Adams back to where Hank is holding some strays," ordered Cord in a tone that defied a negative answer.

The young cowboy reined his pony abruptly away from Stacy and his employer, dug his spurs into the horse's flank and was away at a gallop. Angrily Stacy turned on the forbidding form still beside her.

"You had no right to reprimand him. It was as much my fault as it was his."

"I'm glad you see it that way. It's just what I was thinking too," Cord replied, an amused smile on his lips, but flashing fires in his eyes. "However, if it's any of your business, I was looking for him to tell him just that before I found him with you."

Stacy was more than a little taken back. She had naturally assumed that Cord was disciplining her companion because of Jim's interest in her. The reddening of embarrassment flowed in her cheeks.

"But that doesn't mean I approve of you bewitching my men to such an extent that they forget to do their job."

"I don't know what you're talking about," Stacy muttered.

"You surely don't expect me to believe you were looking for strays on foot in that field?" he questioned.

"No, I don't!" answered Stacy exasperatedly.

"Then there really isn't anything more to be said, is there?"

"Yes, there is!" Stacy exclaimed. "You don't have the right to tell me who I may or may not make friends with."

"I have a great deal to say about it," matching the angry tone in Stacy's voice. "You are in my employ and as such, your actions become my responsibility. If I feel it's necessary, I'll dictate who you may associate with and who you may not."

"Are you telling me I'm to leave Jim alone?"

"I'm telling you that you will not flatter my men and seduce them into having any romantic notions towards you. Is that plain enough?" Cord flashed.

"Perfectly!" she retorted, and kicked her pinto into a canter.

The two silent riders hadn't travelled very far from the meadow when they came in sight of the wizened cowboy driving a half dozen steers. With a wave of his hand towards Hank, Cord wheeled his horse away from the pinto and headed back across the range as Stacy fell in beside the wrangler.

Shortly before noon the small band joined up with the main herd. Stacy searched the riders around the main herd for some sign of Jim, but only caught a glimpse of Cord, which deterred her from looking more closely. She wasn't in the mood for another run in with him. Quietly she followed the wizened Hank to the encampment where they ate lunch and changed horses. Hot and tired, Stacy sat silently astride her horse in the noonday sun and waited for the veteran to join her. He ambled over to the ground-hitched pony beside Stacy and mounted.

"We'll be stayin' with the herd this afternoon," he stated. "The two of us will be ridin' the right flank."

Several times that afternoon Stacy caught sight of Jim, but only once did he acknowledge her presence with a wave. Stacy felt guilty for possibly getting the young cowboy into trouble; she only hoped that Jim wouldn't hold it against her. Of course he couldn't very well rush over when he saw her—after all, he was working. Twice she found herself looking around for some sign of Cord Harris, but if he was taking part in the afternoon drive, he escaped Stacy's eyes. Instead of feeling relieved that his watchful eyes were not on her, she felt empty.

At four o'clock the herd arrived at a stand of cottonwood trees that marked the course of a rushing stream. This was the night's encampment. They drove the cattle across the shallow water, bedding them down on the opposite side. As Stacy followed Hank back over, she looked wistfully at the swift-running water. What an opportunity to wash some of the grit and grime off!

All the hands had gathered around the cook wagon where the coffee was fresh and hot. Stacy and Hank dismounted at the remuda trailers and joined the others. By tomorrow morning the herd would reach the summer pasture and the drive would be over until fall. Stacy stood quietly and sipped her coffee while listening to the boasting and grumbling of the veteran cowhands. Supper would be dished up shortly and she wanted to go down to the stream before then. She finished the last of her coffee and handed the cup to the cook. None of the group paid any attention to her as she walked away towards the cottonwood trees.

Stacy strolled leisurely, following the river upstream. Five hundred yards from camp where the stream widened as it made a turn, she stopped. This was the perfect place to bathe, far enough away from camp to ensure privacy and far enough upstream for the water not to be muddied by the cattle crossing. Even an obliging tree had a lowhanging branch on which she could hang her clothes. Happily she swept the brown hat off her head and pulled out the rubber band holding her hair. Free from the confinement, the long chestnut hair fell caressingly around her shoulders as she sat down by the edge of the water to remove her dusty boots. Her toes wiggled happily in the coarse sand as their owner gazed blissfully at the beckoning water, glistening brightly with captured rays from the sun. Stacy hopped to her feet and made one last glance around her bathing hole to make sure there were no uninvited two-legged visitors, before shedding her blouse and jeans.

Clad only in her undergarments, she waded into the water. A small shudder ran through her at the unexpected coolness of the stream. She hummed merrily as she rubbed away the dirt and grime of the drive. Carried away by her enjoyment, Stacy failed to hear the sound of hooves muffled by the sand. A horse and rider came to a halt beside the overhanging cottonwood where Stacy had hung her clothes.

Still humming her happy tune, Stacy entered the shallower water and began wading towards the bank. Glancing at the tree, she stopped in the now waist-deep water, stunned by the sudden appearance of the horse and rider. Her surprise was quickly replaced by a self-consciousness of her scanty attire. Swiftly she lowered herself into the water.

"You could have had the decency to let me know you were there, Mr. Harris!" she exclaimed, her face red with shame as she addressed Cord's mocking face.

"I missed you at camp and came out looking for you," the deep voice replied, ignoring her angry criticism.

"Well, now you've found me, so kindly leave so I can get dressed." Her embarrassment was replaced by indignation.

"I'll wait for you over there," Cord said, smiling, as he indicated a group of trees where his view of her would be obstructed. Amusement was all too visible on his face as he reined his horse around and left.

Hurriedly Stacy clambered up on the bank, chagrin and resentment hampering her. Trying to dress quickly, she struggled to pull the clothes on over her wet body. The sleeves of her blouse clung to her wet arms and with fumbling fingers she managed to get it buttoned and tucked into her Levi's. The boots slipped on easily even over the damp socks. She removed her hat from the tree and began running towards the place where Cord waited.

Cord stood silent beside his horse observing her approach. The haste with which she dressed and rushed to meet him had flushed her cheeks and her brown eyes were bright with tension and embarrassment. Stacy stopped a few feet in front of Cord and hesitated. Her eyes searched his face, desperately trying to read his inscrutable expression.

"Come on," he said, "I'll walk you back to camp."

A little breathless, she fell into step beside him as he led his horse in that direction. The saturnine face never once turned towards her as they walked in silence. The strain was too much for Stacy. With her free hand she ran her fingers through her damp hair nervously.

"I was hot and dusty from the drive." A hint of defiance was in her voice.

"The water certainly looked inviting," Cord commented, refusing to take the bait of the unvoiced challenge she had made. "To be honest, I was tempted to join you." He searched her face, his eyes travelling from the damp tendrils of her hair around her forehead down her straight nose and coming to a halt at her moist parted lips.

Stacy knew they were very close to camp now. In her side vision she could make out the moving forms of the cowhands. She knew she should feel self-conscious at the possible observance of her and Cord, but she was only aware of the broad shoulders and the strong tanned face of the man beside her. He must have read the confusion and bewilderment in her gaze as she tried to fathom this change in his attitude towards her, for he abruptly released her arm and began their course once again for camp.

"I've never known a woman yet who could turn down a chance to freshen up," Cord teased. For some reason that she could not or would not acknowledge, Stacy felt safer back on their old grounds of mocking banter.

"How can I properly seduce a man if I go around smelling like a cow?" she returned, a new lift in her walk and swing to her head.

"You have a very good point," Cord agreed as they walked into the camp area. "Go grab yourself a bite to eat, little one. I'll see you later."

Stacy felt his hand touch her shoulder lightly as he moved away from her towards the horse vans. The warmth of his touch radiated as she visualized the imprint of his hand on her shoulder. Abstractedly she walked over to the group of men, conscious that her whole attention was focused on the retreating figure. Throughout the meal, she involuntarily watched for his approach. When he failed to come she was depressed. Usually she dreaded his presence, and here she was looking forward to it. What manner of man was he that he could make her want to be with him and hate him at the same time?

The cottonwood trees surrounding the camp hastened the darkening purple of the setting sun. Shadows had begun casting their black forms through the camp. The flickering fires seemed to grow increasingly brighter. From the other side of the flame she recognized the figure of her riding companion of the morning. Jim seemed to be looking for someone as he stood studying the various clusters of hands. Then he spotted Stacy and made his way around the campfire to where she was sitting apart from the others.

"Hi," the serious hazel eyes smiled. "Been looking for you."

"Work hard today?" Stacy asked.

"Not too. I'm sorry I had to leave you in the lurch like that today," Jim said, squatting down beside her.

"We didn't come to blows if that's what worried you," Stacy laughed. "I didn't mean to get you into trouble, Jim."

"Seriously, Stacy, I like you. You know that, don't you?" Jim asked quietly. When she failed to reply, he added, "Are you engaged or anything?"

"No." Stacy avoided the turned head beside her. She should have felt pleased by his affection, but she found herself regretting the turn the conversation had taken. "I like you, too, Jim. You're a very good friend."

"That's the way I feel too," he replied. "I hope I'll be able to see a lot more of you."

"I hope so, too," Stacy said. "I've never had too many friends."

"Stacy," affectionately, a calloused hand raised itself and the fingers caressed her smooth cheek, "you're quite a girl. I bet you could turn a man down and make him feel happy about it!"

CHAPTER EIGHT

"CONNORS!" SNAPPED a voice a few feet away from the couple.

Both Stacy and Jim sprang guiltily apart at the biting tone as Cord stepped out of the shadows. Part of his face was still hidden by the darkness, but there was no doubting the leashed fury in the set of his jaws and the furrow in his brow. His dark eyes narrowed menacingly as he stared at the young cowboy.

"You have a unique talent for turning up when you're not expected," Stacy accused, not liking his dictatorial manner.

"Obviously," was the reply. Cord's penetrating gaze flickered briefly to Stacy and returned to Jim.

"Well?" he demanded.

"I have nothing to say, sir," Jim answered, his chin jutting out as he met the censorious eyes.

Stacy could feel the resentment burning inside her. The way that Cord was humiliating Jim in front of her was unforgivable! His pride was being stripped away right in front of her eyes. How much did Cord think Jim could take? And why should it concern him that she had been talking to the cowboy?

Jim regarded Stacy silently. Finally he bade her good night and walked away. Furious at the tyrannical rancher, Stacy turned to face him, her brown eyes flashing as she trembled from the anger building up inside her.

"Just who do you think you are, Mr. Harris?" she cried. "Do you get some kind of big thrill humiliating a man in front of a woman? Or do you just like everyone to know that you're Mr. Big Shot around here?"

"I don't see where it's any concern of yours what my reasons are," said Cord, his voice still fierce with controlled emotion.

"That's a remark typical of you," Stacy said bitterly. "You consider yourself a law unto yourself, responsible to no one. Well, you're nothing! Do you hear me, nothing! Why, Jim is more of a man than you could ever hope to be. And furthermore, if you think you've succeeded in lowering him in my eyes, you're sadly mistaken. Before, I only considered him to be a friend, but now I can see that, compared to you, he's the only man on earth for me."

"You admit, after all, that it is a man you want," Cord retorted, a muscle in his jaw twitching in his own mounting anger. "I seriously doubt if you would know a man if you saw one."

"I know that whatever it is I'm standing in front of now, it's not a man!" she snapped, fully aware that she was pushing Cord too far, but beyond the point of caring. She enjoyed degrading this paragon before her.

The slender thread that had held his temper in check snapped as his face grew black with fury. Roughly he grabbed Stacy's arms, drawing her so close to him that she could see the throbbing veins on the side of his jaw. The iron grip of his fingers dug deep into her shoulders as she struggled uselessly against his muscular chest. He was much too strong for her. As one large hand moved, sweeping around her waist, the other grabbed her long brown hair, twisting her head back until she was forced to look into his face. Crushed against his chest, she stared tremulously into the now coal-black eyes.

"By God," Cord said hoarsely, "I'll not have you throwing yourself at my men. If it's an affair you're after, well, I'll take care of that right here and now!"

Slowly his face lowered down to hers as if enjoying the apprehension Stacy felt as she realized he was going to kiss her. Valiantly she tried to struggle again, but he restrained her easily. His arm tightened around her as if he meant to crush out every ounce of resistance. As his mouth pressed cruelly against hers, Stacy felt a fire of passion sear through her body. The fierceness of his kiss, meant to punish, hurt, and humiliate, stifled any effort she might have made to respond as the bristle of his whiskers scraped her skin. But the whirlpool of his nearness kept spinning in her mind and the throbbing of her heart must have echoed into his ears as it did in her own. When Stacy felt he would never let her go, Cord stepped away. The suddenness of his release jolted her off balance and she fell to the ground. Stunned, she lay there staring up at the towering figure.

"Never back a man up in a corner," Cord said, the coldness back in his eyes. "I told you once before to learn the rules before you played the game."

"I despise you!" Stacy gasped, rising to her feet and flinging herself at him.

He caught her wrists easily and stared emotionless at the teardrops running down her cheeks. She kicked and scratched at him, but the attempts were warded off easily until she was finally exhausted by her efforts.

"You've beaten me," she finally murmured, fighting the lump in her throat. "You can always force me to do what you want, but you can never make me feel anything but disgust for you."

There was no sign of self-reproach in his eyes as Cord looked at Stacy. As he lowered her imprisoned hands and released them, he stood silently searching her face for what Stacy didn't know.

"I know," Cord finally sighed. "I know. Come on, we'd better join the others."

"Is that all you've got to say?" Stacy asked in a small voice, slightly astounded. "No apologies? If that's the way you treat your woman, I can see why you got jilted."

Cord's face turned to stone at her words and his dark eyes bored deep inside her. Uncomfortably aware that she had trespassed on to something that was none of her affair, the numb Stacy stood there, tear-streaked and proud.

"I don't intend to apologize for my actions. I don't know what you heard about Lydia and me, but whatever it was, it's none of your business," the cold, hard voice replied. "Consider what happened tonight a lesson you should have learned long ago. You're not an unattractive girl. You're lucky that I haven't fallen under your spell or the outcome of tonight could have been quite different. Fortunately, I know you for what you are, and the cheap tricks your kind use to satisfy your egotistical craving for attention and admiration.'' The sarcasm seeped through his words. ''The subject is closed.''

Stacy couldn't speak. She looked into his face, repelled by the disgust mirrored there. Bewildered, she offered no resistance when Cord took her arm and guided her back towards the campfire. Several times she stumbled on the uneven ground, but he never hesitated in his stride. Nor did he even glance her way; only the hand on her arm verified that he acknowledged her existence.

When they reached the campfire, he released her and walked on into the circle without her. Grateful to be away from him, Stacy slipped over to her bedroll, praying no one would speak to her or see her tear-rimmed eyes in the glowing firelight. Hiccupping silent sobs, she crawled into her covers. Cursing him for his unwarranted opinion of her, she snuggled inside the blanket for comfort, but her body and mind retained the memory of the strength and warmth of his arms and the brutality and fire in his kiss. Vainly she rubbed her lips with the back of her hand, but the memory was indelibly marked. Sleep crept up silently on her exhausted body.

THE MORNING sun shone brightly down on Stacy astride the little bay horse she had ridden the first day. She could take no interest in the surrounding country as she rode along the flank of the herd. Listlessly she sat on the pony and let her gaze blur in the multitude of cattle.

Last night in her dreams she had relived Cord's embrace, but this time it was filled with passion and desire. She had returned Cord's kiss with equal fervour. The dream was almost more disquieting than the actual kiss. Afterwards she had clung to him, driven by a desperation that he would reject her. She felt she had somehow betrayed herself in that dream. She hated Cord Harris and everything he stood for. The shame and guilt she felt for the imagined kiss far exceeded the humiliation the actual kiss had filled her with the night before.

The pounding of approaching hooves aroused her from her thoughts. Looking up, Stacy recognized Jim Connors astride the galloping horse. He waved and rode by to pull up beside Hank. They exchanged a few words between them, causing an embarrassing flush to flood Stacy's cheeks as she wondered if they were discussing her. If it had been one of the other days, she would have dropped back to join them, but she was afraid to face them today for fear they could read in her face the events of the night before. A few minutes later Hank rode up beside her.

"We'll be reachin' the pasture in the hour," said Hank. "The Boss told Jim this morning that as soon as we got to the summer pasture you were to go back to the ranch house."

"Why? Did he say?" Stacy asked, dreading the prospect of meeting Cord Harris again.

"Nope. One of the hands will be there with a pick-up and you'll ride back with him. And the Boss wants you to go to his office as soon as you get there," Hank replied, the same searching look in his eyes. "You had another go-round with the Boss last night, didn't ya?"

Stacy started to deny it, but knew she couldn't fool the sharp-eyed cowhand and nodded affirmatively.

"You two do rub each other's fur the wrong way," he smiled with a shake of his head. "Jim said the Boss come up on you two last night."

"I suppose he jumped all over Jim this morning?" Stacy remarked bitterly.

"Jim figured he would, but he didn't say a word about it, in fact he even put Jim in charge of one of the brandin' crews," the veteran smiled, watching Stacy's face closely for her reaction.

"He did?" The amazement was written on her face. "Probably his way of apologizing," she reasoned to herself.

"I imagine you're thinkin' me to be an ole gossip, but are you sweet on Jim or somethin'?"

"No," said Stacy, a hint of a smile appearing on her face. "We're friends. He knew my father, or met him at a lecture."

"Good," the old cowboy grinned with a satisfied gleam in his eyes.

"Good. Why?" Curious at his unusual remark.

"Ain't his type. You need somebody stronger to hold you in check. Fire and fire always makes a bigger flame."

"I didn't know you mixed matchmaking with philosophy, Hank," she laughed. "Tell me, do you have someone in mind?"

"I do, but I ain't tellin'. You'll know soon enough,"
Hank answered mysteriously. Kicking his horse, he
added over the din, "Better get back to work."

Laughing, Stacy joined him, the gloom of the
morning fading in the wake of the sagacious cowboy.
When the last steer had been chased through, Hank
motioned towards a waiting pick-up, indicating that
that was the one Stacy would be taking back to the
ranch house.

She rode over to the remuda trailer and dismounted. Dodging the milling horses and riders, she
made her way to the truck. The driver opened the door
for her and motioned her inside. Stacy exchanged a
few pleasantries with him, but the growing anticipation of meeting Cord after last night's episode gradually silenced her. Her imagination had all sorts of
reasons for his wanting to talk with her. If she was
lucky he might want to put an end to the bargain they
had made.

Driving into the yard, Stacy noticed an unfamiliar
gold-coloured Cadillac parked in front of the hacienda. Even though she wasn't familiar with all the vehicles of the surrounding neighbours, she was sure she
had never seen any car like that before. A curious
sense of foreboding filled her as the pick-up pulled up
beside the house gates to let her out.

Tired and filled with dread, Stacy walked with her
bedroll and hat in one hand and suede jacket in the
other. As she opened the door she wished she had a
chance to clean up and change before meeting the
formidable Cord Harris, but knew that he expected
her as soon as she arrived. Resentment flared briefly

within her, as she recognized that he wanted her at a disadvantage. How could she appear cool and in control if she looked like a dirty urchin?

Stepping inside the cool interior of the entry way, she became aware of voices in the den. Uncertainly she stopped before the closed door and tried to recognize them, but the thick oak door muffled the sounds. "Maybe he's busy and doesn't want to see me now," she thought. No, she might as well get it over with. Resigned, she placed the items in her hands on the bench outside the room, gave a few brisk brushes at the dust on her jeans and blouse, smoothed her long hair back to where it was caught at the neck, squared her shoulders, and knocked at the door.

"Come in," came the muffled reply.

With more confidence than she felt, Stacy opened the heavy door and walked into the room. Cord stood directly in front of her beside his desk. There was a nonchalance and ease in his carriage that intensified her nervousness.

"Come on in, Miss Adams," Cord instructed with a slightly imperious wave of his hand. His mocking eyes flicked over her dishevelled appearance and he added, "I see you've just got here."

"I understood you wanted to see me right away," Stacy said defensively, looking the tall figure in the eye. "If you're busy I can come back later."

"No, that won't be necessary," he said. His gaze left her to travel casually to the tall-backed chair in front of the desk. "You don't mind waiting a few minutes, do you?"

For the first time Stacy's eyes searched the room for the second voice she had heard outside. So intent on meeting Cord was she that she had momentarily forgotten her curiosity about the owner of the Cadillac outside. A movement in the chair captured her attention. The over-sized leather chair with its back to Stacy had hidden its occupant from her view. Now she saw the slender, stockinged legs, the high heels and the polished nails of a feminine hand. As the graceful figure rose from the chair, Stacy felt the quiver of a premonition flow through her. The woman was strikingly beautiful. Her hair was jet black and drawn back into a chignon, emphasizing her high cheekbones and creamy skin. Her eyes, as they turned to survey Stacy, were as black as her hair and sparkled with a subdued fire. She was several inches taller than Stacy and managed to give the impression that she was looking down that graceful nose at her. The dark eyes glowed with pleasure as the woman looked at the bedraggled appearance of the other girl.

"You are going to introduce us, aren't you, Cord dear?" the strange woman asked in a clear, melodic voice.

"Of course," he replied, his eyes never straying from Stacy's blushing face. "Lydia, I'd like you to meet Miss Stacy Adams. She's been helping me around the ranch here, as you can tell. Miss Adams, this is Lydia Marshall, a very old friend of mine."

Murmuring an incoherent hello, Stacy nodded. Lydia—that was the woman Cord had been engaged to! Conscious of the significance of the two being together, she flashed a questioning look at Cord. His face maintained the same mocking expression that she had become so familiar with these past weeks. The gleam in his eyes that she had previously attributed to his satisfaction at her untidy appearance held something more. Maybe they were back together again, but what of Lydia's husband? A thousand questions raced through Stacy's mind as she tried to concentrate on the conversation between the two, but the only thing that remained implanted in her mind after Lydia left the room was the silky voice of the dark-haired woman.

Stacy stared at the closed oak door trying desperately to shake the chilling dread that grew within her.

"I said would you like to sit down, Adams," the deep voice repeated in a slightly louder tone.

"Of course—I'm sorry," Stacy mumbled, further embarrassed by her inattention. She walked over and sat in one of the straight-backed chairs beside the desk. Cord had already seated himself behind his desk and was shuffling through a few papers.

"She's a very beautiful woman. Did her husband come with her?" Stacy blurted out before she realized it.

"No," Cord replied, a whisper of a smile in his eyes and a smug satisfaction on his lips. "It seems Mrs. Marshall is getting a divorce."

"Oh," Stacy managed in a very small voice. Why did it upset her that the two were obviously getting back together?

"Now to get at the reason I called you in here," he started briskly. "It's quite clear that our previous arrangement is not going to work, at least not the way I planned."

"I'm still willing to write you a cheque for any of the damages that I've caused," she volunteered, sitting nervously on the edge of her chair. "I quite understand that you wish to be rid of me now, and I assure you the feeling is mutual."

"I'm afraid you misunderstand," he said, raising one eyebrow. "I still believe you should work your debt out. What's obvious is that you can't take the place of one of the men, or even half of one. Therefore I propose that you handle something more in a feminine line."

"I don't quite understand what you're getting at?"

"As I mentioned to you once before, each spring I have an auction where I sell some of my registered quarter horse stock, Texas-style. That means a barbecue and a party." Cord's eyes were sparkling as he watched the dawning comprehension on Stacy's face. "I'm sure with your country club background you'll be able to organize this year's activity, which will leave me free to take care of the ranch."

"How many people will be here?" Stacy asked, ignoring the veiled sarcasm in his last statement. "When is it going to be?"

"Before the day's over, I imagine several hundred people will have been here at one time or another. The date is set for June the ninth, almost four weeks away," he answered, studying her face thoughtfully. "Now, if you think it's too much for you—?"

"Not at all," Stacy said defensively. "But I must admit I'm curious why you didn't ask Mrs. Marshall to act as hostess and co-ordinator for you."

"It's really none of your business, the reasons for my decision to use you, but I've already said that I wanted you to work your way out, and this seemed the only alternative." His voice had grown cold at her presumptuous statement. "And Mrs. Marshall is going through a difficult adjustment and shouldn't be expected to supervise the preparations for a gathering of this size with the emotional pressure she's presently under. Besides, it wouldn't exactly be proper for Lydia to do so at this time. Of course, I doubt if you would realize that."

"I didn't know that other people's opinions bothered you," she retorted, stung by the masterly way he was protecting his former fiancée.

"It depends a great deal on the people involved," Cord's icy voice replied. "There are some people whose reputation I wouldn't want damaged, and there are some people who aren't going to be around long enough to worry about."

"If you're making some subtle reference to me, I would prefer that you speak your mind," Stacy said angrily. "You've acquired some ridiculous idea that I go around flirting with every man I meet. At least I don't go accosting guests staying in my home!"

"I thought you'd have better sense than to bring that up," Cord snapped in a dangerously low voice. The muscle in his jaw twitched its familiar warning sign again. "Last night is better forgotten. Most women would have had enough pride not to have brought it up again."

"I don't happen to be most women!" Stacy retorted, rising agitatedly from her seat to stand with her hands clasped tightly on the back of the chair. "Evidently you expect me to forget it with a snap of my fingers."

"Frankly, I don't care whether you forget it or not," Cord said, looking up at the slim figure. "Unless, of course, you want a repeat performance."

"That's the last thing I would ever want from you!" Guilt burned across her face as she remembered her response to his kiss in her dream.

"Very well," he said, closing the subject and turning his attention to a sheaf of papers in front of him. "Here are some of the arrangements already made for the sale which you should make yourself familiar with. You may use this den as the centre of your activities. I won't be disturbing you since I take care of most of my paper work in the office. Quite likely there'll be a few details you will want to go over with me. You can contact me at that time. I believe that's all."

His cold tone of dismissal froze the angry words in Stacy's throat. She stood by the chair for a moment, but he didn't raise his eyes from the stack of papers. Briskly she turned on her heel and strode out of the room, giving the heavy oak door an added impetus as it closed. Gathering her belongings in the foyer, she stalked up the stairs to her room, where she flung her bundle down on the floor and stared at her glowering reflection in the dresser mirror.

AN HOUR later, as Stacy was walking out of the bathroom after showering and changing her clothes, she met Cord in the hallway.

"I neglected to give you the keys to your car," Cord said briskly, his cool, dark eyes taking in the freshness of her appearance. "You'll be needing transportation, so I had one of my men bring it over from the cabin. It's in the garage."

"How thoughtful of you," Stacy replied sarcastically.

"I also had a typewriter installed in the den," he added, his eyes narrowing at her tone. "I believe that should take care of the things you'll need."

"I'm quite sure everything is satisfactory," she said, starting to brush past the handsome figure. But his muscular arm shot out and blocked her passage. Stacy's flashing eyes looked up at the darkening face.

"You can wipe that expression off your face," Cord stated threateningly. "A good thrashing would do wonders for a spoiled brat like you."

"Violence is your solution to everything, isn't it?" she answered, not flinching under his penetrating gaze. "Now, get out of my way and let me by."

Shaking inwardly, she pushed his arm out of her way and walked briskly down the stairs. At the bottom of the steps stood the dark beauty of Lydia Marshall, her black eyes icy cold as she watched Stacy walk past her. The ice vanished as Cord made his way down the steps behind Stacy.

"There you are!" Lydia said in her saccharine voice. "I was beginning to wonder if you'd forgotten me. I fixed us a drink. I hope I've remembered how you like them."

Lydia's voice fluttered after Stacy like a flaunting red cape, but she didn't wait around to hear Cord's reply. Hurrying blindly into the den, Stacy leaned against the closed door and waited for the trembling in her knees and the pounding of her heart to return to normal. Why did she let Cord arouse her this way? He never acted the same way towards her twice. One time he was teasing and friendly as he was when he had found her at the river, and the next time he was violent and abusive, as when he had kissed her so brutally. And today he was the Don, condescending and dictatorial, making sure she knew where her place was. As far as Stacy was concerned Cord deserved the icy Latin beauty of Lydia Marshall with her sickening, ingratiating airs. Oh, how Stacy wished for the steadiness of Carter Mills. She was growing extremely weary of being a barometer of Cord's emotions.

Discouraged and weary from the last three days of riding, she crossed over behind the desk and sat dejectedly in the chair and studied the stack of papers in front of her. The image of the tanned hands shuffling through them crossed her mind. Absently she shifted through them, her attention straying at first until the magnitude of the party with all its details began to sink in.

Horror-stricken, she sat in the big swivel chair and went through the papers once more. If he hadn't been so antagonistic she would have explained that she had never given even a dinner party for more than twelve people in her life. What was she going to do now? The memory of his derisive, mocking smile flitted in front of her as she saw herself trying to explain to him.

"Oh, how he'd like that," Stacy thought. "It would really please him to see me fall flat on my face. Well, that's not going to happen. I'll have to work a lot harder than I thought, but if I'm lucky, he'll never see the few mistakes I'll make.''

With renewed confidence she tackled the stack of papers again and began to sort a plan out in her mind.

CHAPTER NINE

THE RED sorrel tossed his flaxen mane in the air and snorted his displeasure at the firm hand curbing his pace.

"Easy, Diablo," Stacy quieted him, but he continued to pull at the bit.

Maybe a good gallop would release some of her tension, Stacy thought. The row she had had with Cord earlier that afternoon had taken its toll on her patience. Two weeks had passed since he had put her in charge of the sale festivities. The co-ordination of all the various activities was a full-time job and exceedingly trying for someone who had never done it before, despite the assistance from the wives of the permanent hands. Stacy had been pleased with the job she had done thus far. She also had the feeling that Cord was satisfied with her work, too. Not that it really mattered what his opinion was, she told herself. But this afternoon when she was going over some of the correspondence with him regarding the preparation of the auction itself, Cord had asked her for the printer's proof of the sales catalogue. Stacy knew nothing about it and confessed her ignorance of it to him.

She could still see the thundering expression on his face when he heard her words. She burned at the memory of his scathing remarks. If only she had been able to explain to him her inexperience in arranging such affairs, but the humiliation had burned too deep to allow any room for further scorn. The man was so callous that he couldn't possibly possess anything that even remotely resembled a heart.

Cord had been gone almost every day since the initial meeting when he had turned the preparations over to her. Sometimes during the day he took time to confer with her, but their conversations were limited strictly to the auction. Stacy didn't know if the ranch work was pressing or if he was merely avoiding spending any time with her. Lydia breezed in several times looking for him, occasionally condescending to consult Stacy for Cord's whereabouts, conveying the impression that he was helping her with the technicalities of her divorce. Usually she found him somewhere, since Stacy often saw them from her window, Cord's head bent low to catch some confiding remark the raven-haired woman made, her arm resting possessively on his. Stacy normally turned guiltily from the window, blushing as if she had been caught in the act of eavesdropping on an intimate conversation. Other times she watched until they were out of sight before returning to her work with an odd sense of depression about her.

She was positive that Cord's continued absence in the evenings was caused by Lydia. Strangely enough Stacy found herself either missing him or dreading his arrival, and she refused to let herself delve into the reasons for her contradictory emotions.

Several evenings Jim Connors had joined her on the veranda, and they had chatted away, discovering many interests in common. Stacy enjoyed the easy companionship of the young cowboy with his ready laughter and undemanding company. It was a vast difference from her tempestuous relationship with Cord Harris. With Jim she felt comfortable and at ease, not worrying about each little word she said and how he was going to interpret it. The friendly relaxed atmosphere that surrounded her when she was with Jim reminded her of the way she had relied on Carter Mills.

Carter. He seemed eons away. Had it only been such a short time ago that she had been with him? His last letter had been chatty and full of interesting tidbits of various mutual acquaintances, but it also held an underlying current of concern that Stacy couldn't ignore. She knew he was waiting for an answer from her, one that she couldn't give. She had difficulty even recalling what Carter looked like; all she could summon up was a blurred image of short, sandy hair and shining blue eyes so unclear that it could have been Jim she was picturing rather than Carter. Maybe the resemblance between the two was the reason she was so drawn to Jim. Stacy really couldn't say. But she had no desire to think on it. She probably would have been better off if she had never come out here, but then she never would have fallen in love with this wild, rugged country. Even in her present circumstances, Stacy enjoyed the closeness of the demanding landscape. Gone was the overcrowdedness, the smog, and the endless blare of traffic; in its place was endless space, fresh air, and the muffled calls of God's creatures.

With a glance at the sinking sun, Stacy remounted the rested horse and turned him towards the ranch house. Her wandering thoughts were brought up short by the knowledge that she had to return before the sun was too far down.

All too quickly they reached the stables. Stacy dismounted and led the docile sorrel through the fence gate to the stable area. Humming contentedly, she didn't hear the approach of the wizened Hank.

"You shore are mighty cheerful," Hank crackled behind her.

The sudden voice startled her. "Hank! You shouldn't do that!" she admonished with a shaky laugh. "You practically scared me out of my boots!"

"You looked so happy and contented that it seemed a pure shame to spoil such a pretty picture," he grinned.

"I thought only the Irish had kissed the Blarney Stone. Seems you people out here must have one of your own," she teased, a sparkle lighting up her brown eyes.

"Pshaw! Ain't nothin' fancy about tellin' a pretty girl she's pretty when all she had to do is look in the mirror an' see," Hank replied with a grunt.

Warmed by the affection of the gnarled man beside her and the caressing rays of the fiery-bright sun, Stacy had a tremendous urge to spread her arms and envelop the great wild, rugged land that had captured her so completely. Instead she raised her face to the gentle breeze and inhaled the fragrant perfumes it carried.

"I love this land!" she exclaimed, ending in a regretful sigh. "I'm going to hate leaving all this behind."

"I thought you didn't like it here?" Hank commented, turning his head away to hide the twinkle in his eye.

"I've never seen anything like it. At times it's so harsh and desolate, but the beauty is still there. Oh, no, Hank, I don't like it, I love it!"

"Humph! If you're so fond of this place, why leave it? Why don't you just move to some part of the country around here?"

"It wouldn't be the same," Stacy replied with a gentle shake of her chestnut hair.

"What's so special about this place, anyway?"

"It's a hundred different things. The sun wouldn't set quite the same. The hills wouldn't be the same colour," she explained hesitantly.

"The sun sets the same anywhere," Hank snorted. Then he turned to her rapturous face, not even trying to hide the gleam in his eyes and added, "What about the Boss?"

"What do you mean?" Stacy queried, stiffening at the reference to the enigmatical Cord Harris.

"Ain't he a part of all this?"

"Of course not! He's—"

"He's the only reason why you're wantin' to stay here at all," Hank grinned, hurrying on before Stacy could voice the protest forming on her lips. "Quit kiddin' yoreself that you're only here to work out the trouble yore horse caused."

"He won't let me go," Stacy cried.

"You won't let yoreself go," Hank answered. "Face it, girl, the only hold he has on you is your heart. You love him. I've known it for a long time."

"No," Stacy said weakly as the gruff words sank in.

"Reckon it's about time the cat was let out of the bag. If you got any guts at all, you'll admit it to yourself."

Stacy stood speechless after the retreating figure. In love with Cord Harris? Impossible! Why, he was the most arrogant, rude, hateful person she had ever known. She hated him! Memories raced through her mind—the racing of her pulse when he entered a room, the torment and pain of his mocking smile, the burning of her skin at his touch. Stacy groaned, remembering the black hair with its wayward lock that fell on to the tanned forehead and the dark, flashing eyes that so many times threatened to consume her with their fire, and the finely chiselled cheekbones with their shadow of a beard, his mouth that had bruised and battered her with his kiss when all the time she had been seeking it, waiting for it.

Impatiently the stallion turned and whickered to the slim, freckled figure. Numbly she led him to his corral, stumbling several times, unable to focus on anything but the vivid picture of Cord etched in her mind. She loved him! This torment that possessed her when he was near was the desire to love which was antagonized into hate by his rejection. As she turned the sorrel loose in his paddock, Stacy allowed the realization to wash over her. How could she have been so blind not to have recognized it before? A bubble of elation filled her as she raced to the hacienda. A flush filled her cheeks; a glow lit her brown eyes; and a smile spread across her face with the warming knowledge of her discovery. Stacy Adams loved Cord Harris, her heart chanted. She wanted to scream it to the world. Breathlessly she threw open the heavy oak door and rushed into the silent hall.

The emptiness stopped her. He wasn't here. He had left with Lydia this afternoon after Stacy had quarrelled with him. The desolation swept over her. How could she have forgotten Lydia with her raven hair and porcelain skin? The divorcée with her dark beauty had returned to Cord, returned to accept the love he had once laid at her feet. It was she he cared for, not Stacy. The excitement of her new-found love had allowed Stacy to forget one vital thing—Cord despised her, despised everything she stood for!

"Get hold of yourself, Stacy Adams," she scolded, wrinkling the golden freckles on her nose at the self-pity that wanted to swallow her. "Your father didn't raise a quitter. Cord thinks you're a feckless girl without an ounce of sense to your name and concern for no one but yourself. You've got to show him before it's too late that he's wrong. At least you can fight for him. You can give that raven-haired witch a run for her money!"

With grim determination Stacy swept aside the waves of melancholy. First things first and the first was washing the dust off from her ride and after that she would dress for dinner. Tonight she'd wear her backless jersey culotte dress with the bold turquoise and emerald design. She had brought it along on a whim, but now she would put it to use.

A spark of combat gleamed in Stacy's brown eyes as she undressed swiftly and stepped under the biting spray of the shower. "Cord," she let the name roll lovingly from her lips. It had the sound of a man, the tensile strength of a whip cracking overhead. The rugged land of Texas had bred a man to match and conquer its harsh terrain. Remembering the strength of his hands, the steel of his arms and the solidity of his broad shoulders, she felt a quiver of passion course through her. If only she could look into his dark eyes and see a desire and a love for her there, how perfect her world would be.

By the time she had stepped out of the shower, she had recaptured the earlier enchantment of her new emotion. With a youthful resiliency she had bounded back with a sureness based on faith rather than common sense. Briskly she rubbed the rough terry towel over her body. Singing happily to herself, she returned to the bedroom where she proceeded to dress with a great deal more care than she had ever bothered with before.

Finished, she stood before the large dresser mirror inspecting her reflection with a critical eye. The brilliant blues and greens of her dress offset the light golden tan of her arms and the sun-bleached highlights in her hair. With a final glance at the satin shoes peeping under the floor-length skirt, she winked a compliment to her reflection and left the room.

With a regalness of carriage that denied the flutterings in her heart, Stacy descended the stairs. The plump Mexican housekeeper was setting the table in the dining room. The confidence in Stacy's face took a little dive when she saw only one place setting. She almost asked Maria when Cord was expected home, but pride wouldn't let her concede the possibility that he wouldn't be returning early. Her inquiries on previous evenings had always been met with a negative answer and she couldn't bear to hear one tonight.

"The señorita looks lovely tonight," Maria bubbled with her usual wide smile. "You have a date with Jeem, maybe, no?"

"No," Stacy smiled as she tried to steel herself against the trembling in her body.

Quietly she seated herself at the empty table and tried to eat the attractive dishes placed before her. But the anticipation that consumed her didn't leave any room for food even though she tried valiantly to show an interest in the fruit salads and cold meats that Maria had prepared so painstakingly for her. Finally, after picking away at a pineapple confection for several minutes and not tasting a bit of it, Stacy pushed herself away from the table. It was no use. The tension and apprehension of waiting had stolen her appetite. She was just too excited to eat. Nervously she rose from her chair and began pacing by the table.

"Do you not feel well, señorita?" the Mexican woman asked, standing in the doorway of the dining room.

"It was really a very good meal, Maria. I just don't have any appetite," Stacy apologized, not wishing to hurt her feelings.

Maria seemed to accept Stacy's explanation and began clearing away the dishes. Stacy watched for a minute, trying to gather the courage to ask Maria if she knew where Cord was.

"You perhaps would like your coffee out on the patio?"

"Yes, that would be nice," Stacy murmured absently. Quietly she started to walk from the room, then stopped and in a nonchalant voice asked, "Do you expect Mr. Harris home early this evening?"

"Oh, no. He went to a cattlemen's dinner. He usually very late," was the reply before Maria bustled off to the kitchen.

Dejectedly Stacy walked through the living room to the large glass doors that led on to the veranda. The hope had washed out of her eyes as she slid the doors open and stood on the cobblestone floor outside.

The loneliness seemed to seep into her bones, quelling all the hope and confidence she had summoned. Restlessly, Stacy walked farther out and leaned heavily against a pillar supporting the balcony above. She struggled desperately to fight the dejection and listlessness that was surrounding her. The pool shimmered darkly in the dim light, a hint of ominousness in its depths. She gazed in the direction of the family cemetery on the gentle knoll above the house, hidden from direct view by the adobe walls. Silently she whispered a prayer to Doña Elena, Cord's grandmother. If she understood how much Stacy loved this country and her grandson, perhaps the ghost of this Spanish woman would intervene on her behalf. But no, that only happened in dreams. Wishing Cord by her side could not make it so.

Absently Stacy heard the sound of steps on the patio. Assuming it to be Maria with her coffee, she remained leaning against the pillar, not wishing the Mexican woman to see the tears that threatened to roll down her cheeks.

"Just put the coffee on the table, Maria. I'll serve myself in a minute," Stacy's voice was uncommonly low, her throat choked by the emotion she couldn't control.

"The coffee's already here. You don't mind if I help myself before it gets cold, do you?" came the reply.

"Cord," she whispered faintly. For a moment, she was afraid her legs wouldn't hold her. In that brief moment he rushed to her side.

"Stacy, are you all right?" His hands seized her shoulders roughly.

"Yes, yes, I'm fine. You startled me," Stacy replied shakily, refusing to look into the probing dark eyes for fear they would see the naked love she felt.

"For a minute there I thought you were going to faint. You were as pale as a ghost. Are you sure you feel all right?" The concern was still in his voice as his tanned hands remained on her arms.

His nearness overwhelmed her. She was so conscious of the rich black cloth of his suit, the brilliant whiteness of his shirt, and his face just inches from hers, that she couldn't look up. She couldn't let him see what he was doing to her. Her eyes concentrated on his left hand, the strong fingers, the dark, curling hairs peeping out from the cuff of his shirt.

"You're hurting me!" Her voice came out weakly as her body threatened to sway against the massive chest that presented itself so invitingly.

"I'm sorry," Cord said, moving abruptly away from her, a briskness returning to his voice. Stacy glanced up, but his eyes were hidden in the night's shadows and she was unable to determine his reaction. Did he consider her a silly city girl afraid of the dark? "I didn't realize I was holding you so tightly," he finished.

Firmly Stacy got hold of herself. She mustn't act like a coltish schoolgirl. After all, this was what she wanted, a chance to be alone with him. The trouble was her tongue was twisted up with the love in her heart. How much easier it would be just to tell him she loved him. Casually she walked up to the edge of the veranda to join him.

"Care for a cigarette?"

"Yes, thank you," Stacy replied, watching the masculine hands holding the cigarette case as they removed another filter-tipped cigarette and lit it for her. The sudden flare of the lighter illuminated the rough features of Cord's face, outlining the lines of tiredness etched around his mouth.

"Maria didn't expect you back till much later. She said you were at a cattlemen's dinner. Have you eaten?" she asked, trying to keep too much concern from showing in her voice.

"Yes," he replied noncommittally.

"Are those type of things usually over this early?" Stacy asked, desperately trying to keep the conversation going, hoping he wouldn't notice her nervousness.

"No, it was still going on when I left." His reply was abrupt and gave Stacy the impression that he didn't feel like talking.

"I imagine you're rather tired. Perhaps you'd rather I left so you could relax?" she suggested, willing the pain to leave her heart.

"You're extremely solicitous tonight," Cord replied, an eyebrow raised quizzically in her direction. "Yes, I am rather tired, but no, you don't need to leave. If you want to make yourself useful you can pour me a cup of coffee."

Without replying Stacy walked over to the table. As she stood bathed in the light from the living room, Cord's low voice carried to her, "You look very becoming in that frock you're wearing."

"Thank you," she murmured, trying to still the trembling that ceased her hand.

"Were you expecting company tonight?" His voice had changed from an indifferent tone to the familiar mocking one.

"No," Stacy said too swiftly, trying to cover the embarrassment that his observation had caused. If only he knew that the only person she expected was him! "I just felt like slipping into something different."

Cord walked over into the light near Stacy. She handed him his coffee, her own dark eyes flicking up to meet his as she did so.

"I was hoping you'd be up," Cord said briskly, moving out of the light where she couldn't study his expression.

"Oh," Stacy cursed inwardly at the breathlessness in her voice.

"I wanted to apologize for this afternoon. You're doing an excellent job on the barbecue and I was unreasonably harsh." He seemed to hesitate as if waiting for a reply, but no words came from her lips. "No harm has been done, and the fault was mainly mine for not advising you about the catalogue."

"No," Stacy rushed, "I should have realized that—"

"Whoa!" Cord laughed. His warm deep mirth thrilled her. "Let's close the conversation before we start a mutual admiration society."

But that's just what I want to do, Stacy thought as she joined the laughter. She felt rather than saw the tension ease out of him as he turned and flicked his cigarette off into the dark. She watched the arc of the glowing embers as it sailed through the air to be lost in the shrubbery. Her long fingers stubbed her own cigarette out in an available ash tray. Cord had moved over to the pillar where Stacy had been standing when he had arrived. She wandered a few feet to the other side of him, her own cup of coffee held caressingly in both hands, enjoying the feel of its warmth to her palms.

"Oh, the stars are out!" she exclaimed as she looked into the velvet sky at the brilliant array.

"Now you've seen stars before," the mocking voice said.

"Yes, but you see, when I was looking out here earlier, there were only one or two dim stars and now there's hundreds," Stacy explained, radiant with her enthusiasm. "It seemed so lonely with no moon and just a couple of stars, but now it's magnificent."

"Tell me something, Stacy," he said, leaning lazily against the pillar, his dark gaze surveying the lithe form beside him, "are you really what you seem? One time you're a dewy-eyed girl enraptured with a flower or a moon or something, another time you're a hot-tempered Irish colleen fighting me tooth and nail, then you're a cool, sophisticated debutante acting out a part like earlier tonight in your fine gown. Which one is the real you?"

"Will the real Miss Stacy Adams please stand up?" she laughed, not wanting to face the serious eyes. But when he failed to join in with her joke, Stacy added as truthfully as she could, "I suppose I'm all those things."

Her eyes tried to read his expression, but his face was in the shadows. He stood quietly for a time until the silence became too much for Stacy and she nervously walked over and placed her cup near the coffee urn.

"Stacy?" There was a hesitation in Cord's use of her name that she couldn't identify.

"Yes?"

"Would you come here a minute?" If only she knew what made his voice seem so different, almost unsure. "I'd like to ask you something, if you don't mind."

Stacy's heart beat wildly as she moved beside the tall figure leaning negligently against the white column. He didn't turn to look at her, but continued to gaze out into the night.

"How can a man go about asking a woman who has had all the material things she's ever wanted and whose beauty ensures her all the attention she could ever desire to share her life with him?" Cord's voice had a briskness of controlled emotion that wrenched at Stacy's heart.

With difficulty she suppressed a strangling gasp. Oh, dear God, she thought, he's asking me about Lydia.

"What can I offer her? A life in a country that she must dislike? A monotonous existence?" he went on derisively. "Just exactly who does the giving and who does the taking in that kind of a situation?"

"I—I would think offering her your love would be enough," Stacy stammered, pain racking her body in silent sobs, her mind reeling and tormented with doubts.

His dark head twisted sharply to scrutinize her face which she had turned to look out into the night so that the grief that was filling her eyes would be hidden.

"Would that be enough for you?" his low voice asked, but he didn't wait for a reply. "And just how would you let your man know?"

"It would be enough for me if the right man asked," Stacy answered, a calmness settling over her heart, knowing his love would be all she would ever ask. She turned to face him, and a serenity radiated from her face as she added, "And if he loved me, he'd know."

A dark hand reached out and imprisoned her wrist, pulling her over beside him. Her breath came in rapid gasps as the dark, fiery eyes bore into hers.

"If he was unsure, how would you go about telling him, Stacy?" Cord's voice vibrated near her hair. She felt his left hand slip behind her waist, coming to rest on the bareness of her back, its contact searing through her body. His right hand released her wrist and travelled up to her white throat to caress the side of her neck just below her ear. She knew she had only to lift her head slightly to his face, but she couldn't. Very gently, his thumb slid under her chin, forcing her head up. Stacy's eyes didn't travel any farther than his mouth that was slowly descending upon her own.

At the first touch of his lips upon hers, she stiffened, not wanting to give in to their gentle demands. But soon, as Cord's ardour continued, she succumbed rapturously—begging, then demanding, the passion coursing her body at the answering hunger in his embrace. Who would have dreamed that Cord would kiss her in this way? Lydia, yes, but Stacy? Lydia! With a start Stacy came to her senses. Cord wasn't kissing her, not with this much passion. He was pretending she was Lydia! Briskly she broke from his arms, standing terrified in front of him, ashamed of what he must surely guess. His face was at first soft as he looked down at her until the panic-stricken expression on her face registered. Immediately Cord's eyes blazed with fire as he turned abruptly away, his immense chest rising and falling at a rapid rate.

"We seem to have got carried away by our conversation," he said roughly, removing a cigarette from his case and lighting it. "Our thoughts were obviously far apart."

With an audible sigh of relief, Stacy realized he was mistaking her submission and acceptance of his kiss as a pretence that for her, he too was someone else.

"Luckily we both know what we feel towards one another, so there isn't any need to feel embarrassed," he added, refusing to look at the unmoving girl beside him.

"No, thank goodness," Stacy replied with a shaky laugh. "It could have proved very awkward otherwise."

She moved a step away from him, her body still trembling uncontrollably from his kiss, the initial magic of his lips destroyed by the knowledge that she was only a substitute for Lydia Marshall.

"I imagine it's getting rather late," Cord said quietly. "I suppose we ought to be turning in."

"I am rather tired," Stacy replied, grasping the straw he offered. "I'll see you in the morning."

With as much poise as she could muster, she walked out of the veranda into the living room. Cord followed a few paces behind, but as he entered the living room the phone rang. At the bottom of the stairs, Stacy heard him answer it.

"Harris Ranch, Cord speaking— Yes, Lydia, I left the meeting a bit earlier than I'd planned. I intended to call you but—" Stacy didn't wait to hear more.

With a cry, Stacy rushed up the stairs. She couldn't bear to hear him talking to Lydia. It was going to be difficult enough to face him tomorrow without increasing her pain tonight.

CHAPTER TEN

THREE DAYS had passed since that fateful evening with Cord. There were faint circles around Stacy's brown eyes and a slight drawnness in the full mouth, indicating the sleepless nights and tension-filled days. Cord had repeatedly ignored her, no longer checking with her every day as he had done before. In fact, twice when Stacy had been out walking and had seen him in the distance, he had changed direction to take himself out of her path. A crushing sense of defeat had closed in on her as she realized that he couldn't even stand to see her.

Abruptly, Stacy rose from the desk, refusing to let the melancholy within her interfere with her work. The sale was only a week away and there was a great deal still to be done. She was grateful that her time would be so occupied with the auction that she wouldn't be able to dwell on her own problems.

There was a light rap at the door to which Stacy called out for whoever was there to "come in". The oak door to the den swung wide to admit the vivacious form of Lydia Marshall.

"I'm not interrupting you, am I? Because if you're very busy, I'll just stay a minute." An effusive quality in her low voice caused Stacy to cringe inwardly.

"No, not at all," Stacy replied quietly, taken aback at the unexpected arrival. "What can I help you with?"

"Nothing really. I just thought you might have time for some coffee and a little chat."

"Certainly," Stacy agreed, wondering what in heaven's name they were going to talk about. "Just a minute and I'll ask Maria to bring some coffee. Would you care for a roll or anything?"

"I hope you don't mind, but I already asked her to bring some on the chance that you would be free," came the quick reply, followed by a throaty laugh that grated the back of Stacy's neck.

"How thoughtful of you," Stacy answered with a smile that didn't quite reach her eyes. Seating herself in the chair behind the desk, she continued, "It's seldom that I have the time to take a coffee break. It will be a pleasant change."

"I thought as much," said Lydia, rising from her chair as the plump Mexican woman entered the room carrying the coffee service. "I'll take that, Maria. I didn't order any sweet rolls. Did you want any, Stacy? I have to watch my figure, so I decline." At the negative nod of Stacy's head, Lydia dismissed the rotund woman with a curt "thank you".

The proprietorial air that Lydia had adopted irked Stacy, and with difficulty she managed to accept the cup of steaming coffee offered her.

"Oh, before I forget," Lydia exclaimed, reaching down beside her chair for her purse, "I was by the printer's, and I remembered Cord mentioning something about needing the proof for the catalogue so I picked it up. I hope you don't mind. He mentioned how hard you were working, and I thought I'd save you a trip into town.''

"Thank you," Stacy said coolly, accepting the pamphlet. "Unfortunately I still have to go into town for some other things. I'm sure Mr. Harris will appreciate it, though."

"Well, I knew how upset he was over it," the smiling Lydia went on. "I hope he didn't get too difficult. I know what a temper he sometimes has."

The familiarity oozed out of Lydia's red lips, no doubt making sure that Stacy fully understood just exactly how friendly Lydia was with Cord. An anger slowly began to burn within her.

"Naturally, he was upset," Stacy said firmly, "as I was, but everything's under control now. It was merely a lack of communication."

"I'm glad to hear it." An icy glare was in Lydia's black eyes. "I offered to help with some of the work, but Cord assured me that, at this time, it wouldn't look right. Besides, he thought you were doing an adequate job."

Stacy's cheeks flamed at the emphasis of the word "adequate". The sickening knowledge that she had been casually discussed during one of their conversations lay heavy within her. The solicitous tone of Lydia's words coated the coldness that was enveloping her heart with a bittersweet veneer.

"Mr. Harris indicated that your present—er—circumstances wouldn't allow you to take too active an interest in the actual arrangements of the affair,"

Stacy murmured quietly, wondering where she found the voice to speak at all.

Lydia's dark eyes narrowed as she smiled and said, "Then Cord did explain a little of the problems we face." With a disconcerted sigh, she went on, "It's common knowledge how we've always felt for each other, despite my foolishness that got me into this mess. I wonder now how I could have been so naïve as to trade in all this for a sun that shines the same on the Riviera as it does here. I assure you, Stacy, it's a crushing blow to discover that to your husband you're no more than another possession to be dressed and displayed like a masterpiece by Renoir. If I hadn't known that Cord had promised that he'd always be here, I don't know how I would have made it this far. I guess it's knowing that my future is secure once again in Cord's hands. And it's just a matter of time and it all will be made official."

Stacy didn't know if she could take much more of this conversation. She didn't want to know all their "wonderful" plans. It was all she could do to contain herself and not jump up and pace the floor in desperation. Why was Lydia discussing this with her at all? Aloud Stacy managed to say something about how wonderful it was that everything was working out for them.

"Yes, it is," Lydia replied, but her eyes were studying the flustered Stacy coldly. "I'm so glad you see it that way. As attractive as Cord is, a lot of girls in your place would have developed a crush on him."

"Mr. Harris and I rarely discuss anything but business," Stacy answered numbly, trying to keep the emotion out of her voice. "It would require a great deal of imagination to read more into his attentions towards me than actually exists."

"You do understand I would dislike seeing you hurt accidentally when it could be so easily avoided. I know Cord feels a certain responsibility for you, and I wouldn't want to see you interpret it wrongly," Lydia smiled smugly as she rose to place her coffee cup near the silver service. "Well, I really mustn't keep you any more. I know you have a lot to do, and if I can help you in any way, please call me."

"Of course," Stacy replied, the smile on her lips stifling the pain in her chest, knowing that Lydia was the last person she would look to for assistance, and had the distinct impression that Lydia knew it.

Glumly she stared at the catalogue proof in front of her. Mechanically she leafed through the pages, her mind racing back to Lydia's words. "Cord feels a certain responsibility for you, and I wouldn't want you to interpret it wrongly." If only she could! If only she could read more into his actions than what they were. Responsibility? He had always acted as if she was a liability. It was a miracle he considered her at all.

Arousing herself from her thoughts, Stacy began rummaging through the drawers of the big oak desk looking for the copy of the proof supplied to the printer. She finally found it in one of the lower drawers and began the task of proof-reading the long list of quarter horses complete with their registration numbers, sires, and dams. It was tedious, but at least it required her full concentration and the floating image of the rugged Cord couldn't distract her. Flipping one of the pages over, Stacy straightened with a start. Mixed in among the papers was a piece of stationery with the letterhead of "Lindsey, Pierce & Mills, Attorneys at Law." The words fairly leaped off the page at her. Shocked, she glanced at the signature at the bottom of the letter. "Carter Mills, Sr.!" What was a letter from Mr. Mills doing in Cord's desk? Drawn by the unexpectedness of the familiar letterhead and signature, Stacy began reading.

It was addressed to Mr. Cord Harris, Circle H Ranch, McCloud, Texas, and started out "Dear Mr. Harris":

> Miss Stacy Adams, the daughter of a client, has rented a cabin located on your property. In writing this letter, I am stepping out of my sphere of authority. I would like to impose on you by asking that you keep a close watch over her.
>
> The recent death of her father, a close personal friend, has left Miss Adams without any living relatives. Her father left her a very substantial income so that she is financially secure for the rest of her life. Unfortunately she has been very pampered in the past. Despite my protestations she has insisted on this self-imposed exile to recover from her grief. A stubborn and strong-willed young woman, her cosmopolitan raising has not prepared her for the rigours of western Texas, nor the dangers a young woman alone may face.
>
> She has refused to discuss the length of her stay, insisting that it is indefinite. I would appre-

ciate it, if it is at all possible, Mr. Harris, if you could persuade her to return. If she will not, I ask you to accept responsibility for her. I have enclosed a cheque which I hope will cover any inconvenience caused. I remain

Sincerely yours,
Carter Mills, Sr.

"No!" Stacy whispered, staring at the scrawled signature at the bottom of the page. The red-tinged eyes that had shed tears so readily before were as dry as her lips as the horrible truth began to dawn on her. The letter explained so many things. Why Cord had been so hostile the first day they met, advising her that she should return to the refuge of the city life she was accustomed to. Why he had felt so responsible when she had taken that fall off Diablo and insisted that she stay at his ranch to recover. And when she was well, the episode with Diablo had conveniently given him an excuse to keep her here. It was also the reason he was so concerned about one of his hands taking advantage of her. It was all so clear now. He had undertaken the job of guardian when she came and that was all she meant to him.

Lydia's words washed over her again, "Cord feels responsible for you." Oh, God, Stacy thought, he must have told her, too. Her humiliation grew clearer and clearer. How he must wish she was gone! Shamed and hurt, Stacy rose from her chair and stumbled around the desk, groping for some release from her misery. No tears fell on the drawn, pinched face as she made her way out the front door. The hurt went too deep to be salved by the shedding of a few tears.

Waves of nausea swept over her as she stared numbly at the buildings and surrounding hillsides. A hesitant breeze fingered the tendrils of her chestnut hair as she stood immobile on the concrete walk.

A plump brown hand touched Stacy's arm. "Are you okay?" came the concerned voice of the housekeeper.

Slowly Stacy turned and managed a weak smile before she replied, "Yes, I'm fine, Maria. I just needed a breath of fresh air, that's all."

"You don't look so good," the Mexican woman shook her head as she followed Stacy into the house. "Maybe you should take a little siesta?"

"I'll be all right," Stacy returned a little impatiently. More quietly she added, "I'm fine, really. It was just a bit stuffy in there."

Pride and a sense of fatalism squared Stacy's shoulders as she went back inside, opened the door of the den, and entered. An unnatural calm had settled over her that walled the pain apart from her consciousness. If she could maintain this stoical control of her emotions, she would be able to face the long week that lay ahead of her. At her first opportunity, she would announce to Cord that she would be returning East as soon as the auction was over. That would release him from any false sense of responsibility that he felt and remove her from his life for ever. Bleakly she replaced the lawyer's letter in the lower drawer and began mechanically rechecking the catalogue.

THAT EVENING Stacy was on her way down the stairs when she saw Cord talking with Maria in the foyer. The starchy freshness of his blue shirt and the sharp crease of his darker blue trousers indicated his plans to be gone that night. Still possessed by the stupor that had engulfed her earlier, she walked up to him. Poised, she stood waiting until his conversation with Maria was finished.

"Did you want to speak to me?" Cord's voice resounded harshly in her ears.

"Yes, if you can spare the time," Stacy returned just as crisply, ignoring the uncontrollable racing of her heart. His dark eyes rested inquiringly on her pale, drawn face.

"What is it you wanted?"

"I merely wanted to let you know that as soon as this auction affair is over, I'll be returning home," Stacy answered quietly but firmly.

An eyebrow raised sharply as his brown eyes hardened speculatively. "This is rather sudden, isn't it?" he said, and without waiting for her reply, added, "I take it you're not asking my permission."

"No."

"I see," Cord snapped. The sharp coldness sent an involuntary shiver through the haggard Stacy. "I didn't expect you'd last this long."

THE MORNING sun was high over the mountains before Stacy wakened the next day. She had cried herself to sleep the night before, but with sleep had come the endurance to face tomorrow. Mechanically she removed her dress, crumpled from being slept in, showered, dressed, and went downstairs for breakfast. As she gazed out the window of the dining room, the distant hills beckoned her. It was the week-end and there wasn't much Stacy could do for the auction. She decided to spend the day riding the hills. She wasn't up to another confrontation with Cord and this would be by far the easiest way to avoid him. With instructions to Maria to fix her a cold lunch, she hurried upstairs to change into her riding skirt and boots.

A few minutes later she was walking out of the front door, her hat swinging from one hand, her lunch in the other. There was no lightness in her step, but her stride was firm. Reaching the stables, she walked to the paddock where the sorrel was held. Diablo danced forward to meet her and nibbled playfully at her arm as she put on his halter.

She waved a greeting to Hank riding by the stables. Thankfully he was busy and didn't stop to chat. His eyes were far too sharp and she didn't want to be put through another ordeal. The niggling sense of defeat was too painful a reminder without talking about it.

Diablo was full of fire, prancing and side-stepping in defiance of his rider's efforts to hold him at a walk. Four people walked around the corner of the stable. Stacy's attention was concentrated on holding the spirited sorrel and guiding him to the pasture gate. She managed a cursory glance in their direction. Two ranch hands were walking in front of Cord Harris and Lydia. A stifled oath came from Cord as he pushed past the hands and ran towards the mounted rider. The sudden movement towards Diablo startled the sorrel, spooking him into a half rear as he tried to turn in the direction of the approaching figure.

Before Stacy could utter a protest, Cord was by her side, grabbing her by the waist and pulling her off the horse while the other hand had a tight hold on the reins of the panicking stallion. Setting her roughly on the ground, he ordered one of the hands to hold the horse.

"What in the hell were you doing on that horse?" he blazed.

"I was going for a ride, if it's any of your business!" Stacy retorted, her own temper rising at the undignified treatment she had just received.

"You're damn right it's my business!" Cord raged, grabbing her wrist and twisting it to force her closer to him. "Isn't one fall enough for you, or would you rather get killed the next time?"

"That was an accident. It would have happened no matter what horse I was riding," her own eyes flashed in anger. "I own that horse. He's mine, and you have no right—"

"I have every right in the world as long as I'm responsible for what happens to you while you're on this ranch," Cord interrupted coldly, releasing her wrist with a scornful sweep of his hand. "And as long as you're on this ranch, you're not going near that devil."

"Thank heavens, I won't be here long!" Stacy returned sharply. Her anger was reaching a point where the powerful, intimidating man did not awe her. "And you'd better think of a way to keep me away from that horse, because he's mine and I intend to ride him any time I please!''

In the background Stacy could see the contemptuous eyes of Lydia Marshall mocking her childish display. But her irritation with Cord's dictatorial manner and his overworked sense of responsibility ignored the malice that glinted through the black eyes. Approaching the small group from the hacienda was a tall man dressed in a blue sport outfit. There was something familiar about his walk, but Stacy's attention was directed back by Cord's voice.

"I'll lock you in the house if I have to, but you're not riding that horse. There's plenty of other mounts available if you want to ride," Cord answered, his voice lowering in an attempt to curb his anger.

"No, thank you," Stacy said sarcastically, turning sharply on her heel to walk in the direction of the dancing stallion.

The raised voices and angry tones had incensed the hot-blooded horse and his flashing white feet drummed the ground in a staccato rhythm. A rolling white eye glanced back to catch a flicker of movement. Pulling at the lead rope held by the ranch hand, Diablo reared slightly and just as swiftly came down and lashed out with his back feet at the unidentified person behind him. But just as quickly, Cord reacted, pulling Stacy away from the menacing hooves.

Holding her back and shoulders tightly against his broad chest, he muttered in her ear, "You are the most stubborn woman I've ever known!"

The sudden and unexpected physical contact with Cord swept Stacy's breath away. She felt her knees

trembling and her heart racing away with his nearness. She could only hope he would attribute it to the
close call she had with the spirited horse. She was too
weak to step away from him, cherishing the strength
of his arms and the mild aroma of cologne from his
freshly shaved face. Cord turned her around, keeping
his hands firmly on her shoulders. His expression was
grave as he unhurriedly surveyed the pallor in her face.

"I've never met anyone in my life who needed a
good spanking more than you," he growled, releasing her and turning to the waiting group.

"Hear, hear!" came the laughing agreement of the
stranger standing beside Lydia.

The happy baritone voice broke through the mist of
tears that had taken possession of Stacy's brown eyes.
Of course! She should have recognized him. With a
broken sob, she rushed past Cord to the waiting
stranger.

"Carter, Carter! I'm so glad to see you," she cried,
throwing herself in the young man's arms. Her voice
was slightly muffled as she pressed her head against
Carter's chest, but her unexpected greeting had
brought Cord up short.

"Hey there, honey," said Carter, surprised at the
affectionate welcome he was receiving. Instinctively,
his hand reached up to stroke the top of her head. "If
I'd known I'd be welcomed like this, I would have
come a long time ago!"

Brushing away the tears that had trickled down her
cheeks, Stacy stepped away and looked up into the
gentle blue eyes. The suddenness of Carter's appearance combined with the unsettling contact with Cord

had robbed her of her control. She realized that Carter had misinterpreted her welcome, but she was too relieved at having someone she could depend on here. His presence represented a refuge from the storm of emotions that was buffeting her around to the point of exhaustion.

"I take it you two know each other," Lydia commented dryly, breaking the silence that had settled over the small group.

Embarrassed by her emotional greeting, Stacy blushed slightly before turning to introduce Carter. She stammered an introduction to Lydia, overlooking an arched eyebrow and smug smile on the woman's face. Lydia offered a smooth manicured hand to Carter and one of her intense gazes while Cord stepped forward to complete the circle. His dark eyes were icy cold as Stacy started to introduce Carter to him, but Carter interposed before she could begin.

"Mr. Harris, I'm glad to meet you," said Carter, grasping Cord's right hand firmly. "I never thought I'd see the day that anyone would be able to refuse to let Stacy ride that horse and make it stick. I want to thank you for myself and my father for looking after her so well."

"I won't mislead you by saying that it was an easy job. Miss Adams is a very strong-willed girl," Cord answered dryly. "Will you be staying long?"

"Only as long as it takes me to convince Stacy to come back with me," Carter smiled, glancing tenderly down at the chestnut head beside him, "hopefully, as my fiancée."

CHAPTER ELEVEN

STACY HAD been covertly watching Cord's face, protected mentally by the young man standing beside her, but at Carter's statement Cord's eyes flashed their fire upon her.

"Isn't it wonderful, Cord?" Lydia gushed, her malicious eyes flicking over Stacy briefly before she smiled up at Cord and took his arm. "What a romantic conclusion for a reunion! It's really just perfect, isn't it?"

"Yes, it is," Cord agreed, but his voice sounded husky as if he was struggling to control his temper.

No one seemed interested in Stacy's answer to the public proposal, not that she would have offered one if she had been asked. But it grated her that everyone was taking an affirmative answer as a matter of course.

"Carter, I'm in charge of the annual sale of registered quarter horses that Mr. Harris has every year. It's this coming Saturday. Will you be able to stay until then?" Stacy asked, anxious to change the subject.

"Oh, Stacy, you don't have to let a little thing like that stop you," Lydia inserted quickly before Carter could answer. "I'm sure it would be perfectly all right if I stepped in for you. After all, it would be an emergency of sorts."

The last sentence was directed more or less at Cord. Stacy had the distinct impression that Lydia was only too anxious to get her out of the way and the sooner the better. It was all Stacy could do to keep a sigh of relief from escaping her lips when she heard Cord's reply.

"It's too late to make any replacements. The sale is too close and it would mean unnecessary confusion. I don't believe it's all that vital that Miss Adams return immediately," Cord answered, his cold eyes turning on Carter as if daring him to disagree.

"No, of course not," Carter added hurriedly. "As a matter of fact, Dad gave me a week to persuade you to come back with me. We'll just call it a little vacation." The young lawyer exchanged a conspiratorial smile with Stacy before turning back to Cord. "Is there a hotel in town where I could stay? I'd like to get settled in."

"There's no need to stay in town," Lydia began.

"No, you can stay here," Cord interrupted, silencing the polite protest Carter had started to make with a wave of his hand. "There's plenty of room at the hacienda. If you'll excuse us, I have some work to do, and I believe you mentioned that you had a luncheon engagement, didn't you, Lydia?"

With a firm hand on Lydia's elbow, Cord manoeuvred her away from the standing couple. Silence descended over Carter and Stacy as he surveyed her quietly.

"You never did answer my question. It wasn't exactly a question, though, was it?" the soft voice asked. "Don't answer it now either. I'll ask it again later when the setting is a little more romantic. Right now you can direct me to my room and tell me all the 'tall Texas tales' you've learned."

With a nervous laugh, Stacy joined hands with Carter before moving towards the hacienda. Eagerly she related the happenings since her arrival, many of them taking on a humorous aspect on their recounting. Entering the adobe building, she ushered him to one of the spare rooms down the hall from hers, after suggesting that he meet her at the pool in half an hour.

Stacy was floating lazily on her back in the pool when Carter surfaced from his dive beside her. The pair swam round for an hour before pulling themselves up on the side, happy and exhausted.

Stacy studied Carter's lithe, tanned body through lowered lashes. His light, almost blond hair was still wet from the swim and his smooth, unlined face seemed unusually young when she compared it to the rugged, sculptured features of Cord. Soberly Stacy realized Carter wasn't as indomitable as he had seemed before, but she had fallen easily into their old comradeship, unable to let him know the change that had taken place in her, the difference in her thinking.

"I know about the letter your father sent to Mr. Harris before I came out here," Stacy said quietly, and noticed that Carter had the grace to redden.

"You understand that Dad was concerned about you," Carter commented, squinting his blue eyes at the sun. "As it turned out, we can be glad he did. I didn't know anything about it until after you were hurt." Turning to study Stacy, he asked, "What made you stay here—this auction?"

With as little detail as possible, Stacy explained the incident with Diablo, glossing over as much as she could Cord's antagonistic attitude towards her. Mischievous amusement spread over Carter's face when she finished, taking an impish delight at the implied humiliation.

"Imagine you out there chasing cows! That's too much!" he chuckled.

"Well, it wasn't too funny at the time," Stacy retorted, unable to keep from bristling at his teasing. "You don't exactly have a choice when Mr. Harris issues an ultimatum."

"I rather got that impression this afternoon," Carter said, sobering slightly, but a devilish gleam remaining in his blue eyes. "I don't think patience is one of his virtues."

"Hardly," Stacy replied grimly. "And he certainly doesn't have any patience where I'm concerned. I still think it was beastly of your father to write that letter, especially without telling me. When I remember some of the terrible things I said and did because I thought Cord was nothing but an arrogant tyrant who enjoyed ordering people about—"

"You mean he doesn't?"

"No. That is—" she stammered, struggling to find the right words to explain her change of attitude without giving her true feelings away.

"Never mind," Carter laughed, rising to his feet. "I don't care what he is or does. He managed to keep you off that horse and in one piece until I could collect you. For all I care he could be Billy the Kid. Now, I'm going to change before this Texas sun of yours turns me into a lobster."

THE FOLLOWING night, as Stacy dressed for dinner, she dreaded the evening to come. She had hoped with Carter here that she would be able to put Cord in the back of her mind, but Cord had very successfully squashed that. Since her brief conversation with Carter alone the previous afternoon, Cord had been around constantly. If he didn't actually take part in their conversations, he was in an adjoining room. Either way his presence thwarted any attempts for privacy that Stacy and Carter might have made.

Carter had jumped at the dinner invitation when Stacy passed it on to him. His enthusiasm coupled with her earlier agreement left no way for her to back out. The anguish Cord's nearness would surely cause made her wonder if she derived some sort of bizarre pleasure from her torment. Each day that went by brought her closer to the time she would leave for good, thereby turning each glimpse of the virile man into a cherished memory to last the eternity she would be alone.

Willowy and delicate, like something out of a misty dream, Stacy descended the stairs to where Carter Mills and Cord Harris waited in their white dinner jackets. Carter didn't speak, but the admiration in his blue eyes sparkled a compliment that was more eloquent than words. Hesitantly Stacy looked into Cord's face for an affirmation of Carter's approval, but the dark eyes were masked and his opinion unrevealed, while the agitated twitching of the jaw muscle marred the still, stone-like quality of his brown face. Regretting that she had sought his praise, Stacy turned back to her escort.

"Are we ready?" she asked.

"And willing," smiled Carter, possessively clasping his other hand over the delicate one on his arm.

A sleek and shiny brown Continental was parked in the drive. Stacy slid into the back seat behind the driver and waited nervously for Carter to walk around the car to join her. Apprehensively she glanced into the rear-view mirror to meet Cord's dark, enigmatical eyes that quickly looked away. The fair lawyer climbed in beside Stacy while Cord started the motor and manoeuvred the luxury car out of the drive. The conversation was sketchy during the journey to Lydia's, with Stacy too conscious of the dark head in front of her to do anything but pretend an interest in the scenery racing by.

"You're very quiet tonight," commented Carter after they had parked and Cord had gone into the house to collect Lydia. "Is something wrong?"

"No, of course not," Stacy returned, a grateful smile on her face for the concern in Carter's eyes. How could she explain that the proximity of the driver upset her? "I enjoy looking at the land, especially when the sunset is so close. It gives everything a mysterious peace."

"That's my girl," Carter muttered with a mocking shake of his head. "Here she sits beside a man who's

travelled halfway across the country to see her and
she's admiring the scenery.''

"Oh, Carter, you know I'm glad you're here,"
Stacy laughed, fully aware of the comfort his presence was to her.

"But I wonder if you're glad because it's me or because it's an old friend." A sad, serious expression was
in his blue eyes as he gazed at her astutely.

Stacy's protest was arrested by the approach of a
white-jacketed Cord with Lydia clutching his arm.
There was a satisfied smile on his face as he gazed
down at the chic woman. Stacy's heart experienced a
painful tug as her brown eyes flashed a jealous green.
Lydia's raven black hair fell loosely about her creamy
white neck, accenting the sensuous décolleté of her li-
lac satin gown hanging precariously by two slim
rhinestone straps.

As pleasantries were exchanged, Lydia glanced at
Stacy's ring hand and then looked at Carter petu-
lantly. "I thought we were going to have something to
celebrate tonight. Or did you forget to bring a ring
along to make the announcement official?''

Carter managed a joking, noncommittal reply
which escaped Stacy, whose attention was caught and
held by Cord's intense gaze in the mirror. She felt the
colour rising in her cheeks at the inquisitive and derisive expression in his deep brown eyes. Unwilling to
take part in the conversation between Lydia and Carter, Stacy again forced her attention outside the glass
windows. She managed to keep the jealousy and bitter pain from showing itself for Cord's mocking eyes
to see.

Arriving at their destination, Stacy became enchanted with the rambling two-storey building nestled in a sylvan setting of pine trees and lush greenery. As the foursome entered the restaurant area, the host greeted Cord by his first name and ushered the group personally to a secluded table.

Carter held out the chair on Cord's left for Stacy, his hand lingering briefly on the filmy silk covering her shoulder. The reassurance of his touch quieted the nervous tremor in her heart. With a still hand, she raised her champagne glass with the others as Carter made a toast.

"To Texas."

"And the happy reunion of those who've been separated," Lydia added, her gaze taking in Cord's profile possessively before turning to include the other couple.

Stacy was relieved when the dinner was served and over. At least in the lounge the entertainment would force conversation to the minimum. Leaving the table, Stacy and Carter followed the other couple into the lounge. Stacy's eyes were riveted on Cord's dark hair curling above the collar of his white dinner jacket. As if conscious of her inspection, he turned, gazing mysteriously for a moment into her startled brown eyes before speaking.

"I hope you won't be too disappointed in the band. The group is mainly Mexican in extraction, so you'll find the music has a Latin-Western flavour rather than the beat you're accustomed to."

Inwardly Stacy flinched at the subtle undertone of censure that laced Cord's words. His opinion of her was so low already that it seemed useless to protest this statement. Without replying she and Carter followed them to a table. As soon as the cocktail waitress had taken their order, Carter asked Stacy to dance. She quickly obliged, happy to leave the disconcerting company of Cord and Lydia. Three guitars played the strains of an old ballad to the gentle tempo of drums. As she matched the familiar pattern of Carter's steps, a spray of confidence returned to Stacy.

"What's the matter with you tonight?" Carter asked suddenly, his blue eyes examining her face intensely. "I have the feeling you're afraid or hiding something."

Startled by his unexpected frankness, Stacy missed a step. A numbness seized her throat as hundreds of protests flashed through her mind, but before she summoned one, Carter went on.

"I don't think I want you to answer me. I think you'd lie or maybe not tell me the whole truth." His tone was extremely serious. "It would hurt too much either way. Stacy, if you ever want to tell me what's wrong, I'll be here no matter what."

"Carter, I—" Stacy began, tears of misery welling in her brown eyes.

"Sssh! We won't talk any more. Maybe later when we're alone, but not now," he whispered in her hair, and drew her closer into the comfort of his arms.

When the last strains of the ballad faded away, the group struck up a bouncier tune and the young couple remained on the floor. The knowledge of Carter's affection gave Stacy a crutch to cling to and the ability to return to the table with a more sincere smile on her face. Despite the invisible support of Carter, the evening dragged. The mocking tone and twisted smile of Cord whenever he addressed her made Stacy nervous and the triumphant glitter in Lydia's eyes fanned the ache that throbbed so close to the surface. The envious lump in her throat swelled whenever she watched Cord dancing with the sultry black-haired woman. Towards the end of the evening, Carter asked Lydia to dance, leaving Stacy alone with Cord.

"They dance well together," Stacy commented with an attempt at nonchalance as she watched Carter and Lydia fall into step. Cord gleamed back at her, an unamused smile that flickered briefly with an emotion that Stacy couldn't quite recognize.

"Jealous?" the low baritone voice spoke. "Lydia is a very beautiful woman."

"No, of course not," Stacy returned, but there was a tremulous catch in her voice as she spoke. She was jealous of Lydia, but not for the reason Cord was thinking.

"Shall we dance?" Cord asked softly as he rose and stepped behind her chair.

Naturally she would refuse. Why punish herself further by being held in his arms when he desired another? What could it possibly accomplish but more heartache? But not a word of protest had passed her lips as she found herself in his arms on the dance floor. There was no retreat now and the glow that radiated unconsciously from her upturned face laughed at the recrimination of her conscience. The firm hand on the small of her back was strangely exciting and the tender brown eyes that looked down upon her made her

heart race with uncontrollable happiness. At this moment it didn't matter whether he was dancing with her
out of pity or courtesy. Her hand tightened impercep-
tibly in Cord's and with a gentle smile in his eyes he
drew her closer to his broad chest until her brown head
nestled against his shoulder. Ignorant of the melody
of the song the band was playing, the conversation of
the dancers around them, oblivious to anything but
the thrilling nearness of Cord, Stacy danced in silence, capturing the sensation of the rhythmic sway of
his hips, the gentle pressure of his body against hers,
the firm clasp of his hand and the caress of his breath
on her hair.

The dance over, as if by previous arrangement,
Cord immediately suggested calling it an evening.
Torn apart by the emotions that threatened to surface
from his nearness and the hopelessness of her love,
Stacy quickly agreed.

THE RIDE home had been a silent one. Looking back
on it two days later, Stacy tried to analyse the reason.
Carter had been unusually quiet. In the past they had
often spent hours without talking, but this time there
was an uneasiness about him, as if he was grappling
with a problem he didn't know how to handle. And
Cord had answered Lydia's sentences so abruptly that
even she fell to silence. It had been a relief when the
Continental had finally turned into the ranch drive
and Stacy had escaped to the sanctity of her room.

Carter had been his old self the next morning,
laughing and joking as before. After volunteering to
help Stacy with the auction arrangements, he had

pitched in with a familiar gusto, running errands into town, checking with Hank regarding the yearlings, and taking some of the more time-consuming tasks off Stacy's hands. Cord had reverted to his old habit of unexplained absences. The past two days he had practically avoided Stacy and Carter, joining them only once for dinner Monday evening and leaving immediately afterwards. He had not mentioned where he was going, but later that evening Stacy had seen a light burning late at the ranch office. Lydia hadn't been over either, which surprised Stacy as the divorcée had almost become a fixture at the ranch since her return.

Removing the paper from the carriage of the typewriter, Stacy forced her thoughts to return to the business at hand. Her morning had been consumed with last-minute requests for circulars of the auction. This one was finally the last. Slipping the information into an envelope and stamping it, she placed it with a stack of similar letters that awaited Carter's return from the stables. If she was lucky she would have time for a cup of coffee and a cigarette before she had to meet the wives of the ranch hands to go over various details they would be responsible for during the barbecue.

Leaving the den, Stacy walked towards the kitchen to help herself to some coffee. But Maria appeared in the archway between the dining room and living room carrying a small tray with a steaming cup of coffee and a sweet roll on it.

"You are a life-saver," Stacy smiled. "I was just going to the kitchen to get myself a cup."

Maria bubbled her pleasure before adding, "Weel the Señora Leedia be joining you?"

"Lydia?" Stacy's tone puzzled.

"*Si*. She just drive up een her car. I theenk perhaps she dreenk too."

"I don't know—" Stacy began, but was interrupted by the opening and closing of the front door.

"Stacy, good morning. I'm so glad to see you're not busy," Lydia smiled, entering the living room as Maria left. "I hoped to have a little chat with you today, but I was afraid you'd be all tied up with Saturday's affair."

"I'll have to be running off in a few minutes," Stacy replied, not anxious to have another "little chat" with Lydia. Their previous discussion was regrettable enough without enduring another.

Gracefully Lydia seated herself in the chair opposite Stacy, smoothing the skirt of her elegantly styled sundress before speaking. "I don't see any engagement ring. Surely you've put that poor boy out of his misery by now."

"If you mean Carter," Stacy said coldly, incensed that Lydia was meddling in something that was none of her business, "I've been rather busy lately. There's no rush, is there?"

"I wouldn't let him get away from you, if I were you."

"That's the point, though, isn't it? You're not me."

Lydia's cold eyes flickered ominously for a moment at Stacy's words.

"That's true, but I do have a better view of the situation than you," she suggested solicitously.

"Why don't you come to the point?" said Stacy, irritated by the phoney concern that Lydia was attempting to project. "We could talk in circles all day. Fortunately I have better things to do."

Surprised at Stacy's unexpected audacity, Lydia rose from her chair, walked behind it, then turned her dark head with its glistening coronet of braids towards her.

"You're quite right," her tone was sarcastic and contemptuous. "There's no love lost between us, so why pretend? My point is really quite simple—don't withhold your answer from Carter in the hope that Cord will come through with a better offer, because he won't. Do you think that Cord is so blind that he doesn't realize that you've fallen in love with him?"

"Afraid of a little competition, or is your hold so slight over Cord that you can't take the chance?" Stacy retorted, standing to meet the glare of the older woman's challenge.

"Don't be ridiculous!" Lydia exclaimed. "A more mature woman would be able to recognize the difference between affection and pity. You moped around all Sunday evening and then lit up like a Christmas tree the minute Cord danced with you. Can't you tell that he feels sorry for you, that his over-active sense of responsibility forces him to do these things? I don't know where your sense of pride is or whether you haven't outgrown that cow-eyed teenage stage yet, but either way your presence has managed to influence the plans that Cord and I have made. As ridiculous as it sounds, he doesn't feel he should make his true feelings known for fear of hurting you."

"As I told Cord and I'll tell you, I'm leaving right after the auction," retorted Stacy. "I'll be returning with Carter, so that should end your concern. In a few more days I'll be out of your lives for ever and you and Cord can do whatever you like. In the meantime, I prefer that you leave this house now and stay out of my way in the future," Stacy's voice trembled with controlled anger. But the truth of Lydia's words cut deep.

The click of triumphant heels echoed through the living room as Lydia left. Numbly Stacy heard her satisfied tone as Lydia exchanged greetings with Carter just entering the house. Walking into the living room, Carter studied Stacy for a second, noting the clenched fists at her side.

"What happened? She looked as if she just tried on the glass slipper and it fitted."

"Really?" Stacy remarked with unnatural bitterness. Seeing the formation of a question in Carter's eyes, she hurried on, "I have a meeting now. There's some mail lying on my desk. Will you see that it gets out today?"

Gathering her notebook, she hurried out the door.

THE FOLLOWING evening Stacy and Carter went for a late ride after dinner. On their return Stacy chattered away happily with Carter refreshed and relaxed by the sunset ride.

"If you don't mind, I'm going to wash off some of your precious Texas dirt," said Carter as they reached the front door of the hacienda. "I'll meet you on the patio for a drink in half an hour."

"A deal," Stacy smiled, preceding him upstairs to her own room.

A short time later she joined him on the veranda. He was sitting quietly on one of the settees rubbing the ears of the German Shepherd abstractedly as he stared off into the deep ebony of the night. Seeing his mistress, Cajun pattered happily over to her side as Carter rose to meet her. Taking the hand extended to her, the chestnut-haired girl contentedly let herself be drawn into the settee beside him.

"It didn't take you very long," Carter smiled. "I thought I'd be able to sneak in an extra drink before you got here," indicating a tray of tall glasses on the side table.

"At least you saved one for me," Stacy teased, cradling an icy drink in her hands as she gazed into the midnight curtain of evening. "It's a gorgeous night. I wonder where all the stars are?"

"If I were a proper lover, I would say they were all in your eyes."

"Oh, Carter!" Stacy laughed protestingly, leaning against the back of the cushion.

Tenderly he cupped her chin in his hand, his face sombre in its study of her sobering expression.

"I wish I could say that and know it to be true," he said, releasing her and rising abruptly.

Stuffing his hands in his pockets, Carter walked over by the pillar and gazed into the distance. Stacy fidgeted nervously with the pocket on her orange and yellow shift. The truth of his statement brought back the despair she fought so hard to subdue.

"Do you know how I've planned for this evening ever since I arrived?" A strange, bitter quality was in his voice that Stacy had never heard before. "Here we are, all alone with not a soul to bother us. The setting is perfect, the black night shutting out the world, a couple of stars winking their encouragement, and a beautiful girl, her dark eyes filled with anticipation at the words that are to be said." The light brown head turned to look back at Stacy. "Only your eyes aren't filled with anticipation, are they?" He looked down at her.

Salty tears trickled down her cheeks to her tightly pressed lips as she bent her head from his accusing blue eyes.

"I was going to do it all properly tonight—get down on my knee and say, 'Stacy, I love you and I want you to be my wife,'" said Carter, his voice almost a monotone. "Corny, isn't it? I love you, but you see, I'm a proud man. I don't want to possess something that doesn't belong to me. I suppose there are men who would have asked you anyway and taken the chance that they wouldn't be turned down. I'm not asking for an entirely different reason. I'm afraid you might accept, and I couldn't live with you knowing that you're in love with some rancher in Texas."

Shame and humiliation shook Stacy's slim shoulders at the pain and bitterness she had brought into Carter's world. Rousing out of his mist of self-pity, Carter looked at the silent, sobbing form and walked over to where she sat, a hand moving unsurely towards her head.

"Oh, Stacy, why, why does it have to be this way?" His voice choked as he swept her off the chair into his arms.

"Carter, I wanted to tell you, but I couldn't," she moaned into his shirt. "I couldn't hurt you, not when I knew what that pain was like."

"It'll be all right," he smiled, drawing comfort from the easing of her pain. "You know the saying 'It only hurts for a little while.'"

"I wouldn't have said 'yes'. I wouldn't have done that to you."

"No, I think I knew that," holding her away from him as he wiped her moist cheeks with his hand. "Inside I knew you were made of a stronger stuff."

"You will stay," Stacy asked, "and take me home after the weekend?"

"Of course. Don't you know, my pet, that you can use me any time?" Carter grinned, his smile taking the sting out of his words.

"I don't know what I would have done if you hadn't come when you did. I hadn't the pride to leave nor the strength to stay," she confessed, nestling under his arm as they walked towards the yawning light from the glass doorway.

A troubled sigh echoed her words as Carter stepped forward to open the door. Hesitating just inside, Stacy turned to wait for him. He had stopped a step behind her, his attention riveted ahead of her. The brittle iciness of his blue eyes startled her and she turned to where he was looking. Cord was standing slightly to her right, a book in one hand and a cigarette in the other. His dark eyes were narrowed in an inscrutable expression as he looked past Stacy to Carter. Abruptly, Cord turned his head and walked over to an ash-tray where he snubbed his cigarette out viciously.

"You young people are turning in rather early to-night, aren't you?" he taunted.

"It's been a hectic day," Stacy murmured, starting to the stairway.

"All the arrangements are going along smoothly for the sale on Saturday, aren't they?"

"Of course. If you'd like to go over them now—" Stacy began, stung by the hint of neglect in his words.

"No, that won't be necessary," Cord interrupted, his dark eyes examining the pinched lines in her face. "There's time enough in the morning." His tone curt and dismissive.

"Good night, Mr. Harris," Carter offered, a little sarcastically.

"Yes, good night, Cord," Stacy hastened at the sharpening of the rancher's eyes.

"Good night." His voice followed them out of the room.

CHAPTER TWELVE

"HELLO!" CAME the call from the hill.

Stacy looked up in answer to see Carter's long legs carrying him down towards her. "Hi yourself," she replied with a grin.

"I should have known I'd find you down here," Carter reproached. "Don't you realize what time it is? You've been going since eight this morning."

"It's only half past seven and I have a few things to finish up before tomorrow," Stacy replied, ignoring the mild rebuke in his voice. "Linda and Diane decided to set up the tables tonight instead of tomorrow morning. I thought I'd give them a hand. Did you get the things from Molly that Mrs. Grayson needed?"

"And delivered to her already. She shooed me out before I even got to sneak a taste of her famous barbecue sauce," Carter concluded with a mock grimace. "What's left to do?"

"Nothing, I hope," Stacy answered with a nervous look around at the long row of folding tables. Waving a good-bye to the two women who were walking away, she turned to Carter apprehensively. "Tomorrow will tell the tale. All my mistakes will be blatantly obvious."

"Where's that girl who always rolls with the punches?" Carter teased with a twinkle in his eyes. Wrapping an arm around her shoulders, he turned her towards the hacienda, adding, "Day's done. Let's go and have something cool to drink."

Stacy laughed in spite of her nervousness. A little relaxation would be in order, especially in the face of the ordeal ahead of her tomorrow. A twinge of pain laced her brown eyes as she considered what this week would have been like if Carter hadn't come. Studying his tanned face out of the side of her eye, she examined the new lines at the corner of his lips. Outwardly there was no change in Carter's attitude towards her and no reference had been made to Wednesday's ill-fated evening.

"Regretting the end coming?" Carter asked quietly, his hand squeezing her arm in comfort.

"No," Stacy sighed. "I'll be better off when I'm away from here." And only haunted by Cord's memory, she added to herself.

The couple skirted the front entrance, going directly to the patio at the side of the adobe structure. While Stacy settled herself on one of the chairs, Carter entered the house to get the drinks. The lowering fiery globe of the western sun failed to lighten Stacy's darkening brown eyes as she gazed around her morosely at the surroundings that had become her home these past few weeks. Drawn by a compulsion she didn't understand, she found herself staring intently at the knoll rising above the house. Distantly she heard the phone ringing in the living room and Carter answering it. Numbly she rose and began walking towards the small hill and the as yet unseen cemetery at the top. She didn't hear Carter call her name nor see his still form standing on the cobblestoned veranda with their drinks in his hands.

She didn't stop until she reached the black, wrought-iron fence that enclosed the graveyard. Ignoring the smaller crosses and markers, she made her way directly to the stone bearing the words "Elena Teresa Harris." Slowly she knelt in front of the tombstone until a denim knee touched the earth. One brown hand reached out tentatively and traced the letters gently. Two bright tears trickled down her cheeks as Stacy tried to draw comfort from those Cord had loved. Grief and anguish gripped her heart as she leaned against the silent grey stone.

Again Cord's voice echoed in her ear, but this time it sounded so real that she turned her brown head to look. Her eyes had to be playing tricks on her, for there before her stood Cord. It had to be a dream because when she looked up into his face there was the most peculiar light in his eyes. Suddenly Stacy became conscious of the encroaching shadows among the graves. Looking quickly to where the sun had been, she saw only a crimson glow marking its departure. She wasn't dreaming! The realization that it really was Cord standing before her jumped into her eyes as she turned back to face him. At the change in her expression, the large muscular arm that had started to extend itself towards her returned to Cord's side as she hastily scrambled to her feet.

"What are you doing up here?" Cord questioned, a hint of the softness remaining in his voice as he surveyed the pained, almost guilty look on her face.

"I came up here to—" The truth of her intention almost escaped her lips before Stacy could stop it. Nervously she glanced to the grey stone that marked the grave of Doña Elena before her eyes slid to the marker beside it. "Your father's grave," she ended lamely, conscious of the narrowing eyes upon her. "I was remembering my father and somehow I thought coming up here would make him seem closer."

Whether he accepted her muffled explanation or not, Stacy couldn't tell. Gripping her arm in his hand, he steered her out of the small cemetery without any further comment. Uneasily Stacy glanced into his face. Whatever he was thinking wasn't reflected there. The few minutes of silence were unbearable for her.

"How did you know where I was?"

"Your boy-friend saw you walking this way," Cord answered, sarcasm seeping through his voice as his long strides carried them down the hill.

"Oh," Stacy added faintly, as the steel grip propelled her before him.

She permitted herself a quick look down to the veranda before returning her concentration to the uneven ground beneath her. When they reached the edge of the cobblestones, Cord released her arm as if in distaste. A tight-lipped Carter handed Stacy her drink, his blue eyes examining the white pallor of her face.

"Are you okay? Where were you?" he asked quietly.

Stacy managed to nod an affirmative to the first question before Cord interrupted her. Swallowing a big drink from his glass, he stated in his derisive mocking tone, "She was using my father's grave as a stand-in for her own."

Carter's blue eyes studied Stacy's intently for a brief second before dismissing the explanation. But Cord wasn't finished.

"Giving in to self-pity is a luxury that this land doesn't allow, not for the people who live here." The cold harshness of Cord's dark eyes penetrated Stacy's heart, sending the blood rushing to her face from the wound.

Cord turned away and started walking towards the area north of the stables where the preparations for the barbecue were going on. Stacy and Carter followed a few steps behind. None of the three spoke on the way. Cord seemed to ignore the fact that they were behind him and Carter only glanced Stacy's way once.

The trio passed the long lines of tables gleaming eerily in the waning light and continued towards the red glow emanating from a nearby stand of greasewood trees. Cord slowed his pace so the three approached the fire at the same time. A long pit had been dug in the grove and a fire started in it. In the hazy glow, a form moved to shove another log into the fire. Stacy recognized Hank with a smile.

Adjusting her eyes to the flickering light, she studied the ingenious arrangement of the barbecue with interest. Curiosity overwhelmed the feeling of tension that had previously held her silent. "Are those old beds the meat's on?"

"Army cots," Cord smiled in answer. "We wrap the legs in foil to retain the heat. The hands take turns tending the fire through the night and basting the meat with barbecue sauce."

"Heavens!" Stacy exclaimed as she saw the enormous amount of meat on the metal slate. "Aren't you going to have too much to eat?"

"We Texans have big appetites," Hank snorted. "We don't mess around with those tiny sandwiches like folks back East. If yore gonna sit here and watch the fire, I'll get some other things done," he finished. As he turned away from the fire, he added to Carter, "Might as well come along and give me a hand, I ain't as young as I used to be."

Without waiting for an answer he tottered off into the dark. A twinge of fear clutched Stacy as she realized that Hank intended to leave her alone with Cord. She knew Carter was staring at her, waiting for her to say something to indicate that she didn't want him to go. She couldn't think of anything to say. With a stifled exclamation, Carter stalked off through the trees after Hank.

Cord was the one who finally broke the silence, his low voice drawling out, "Well, you'll be leaving in another day. I suppose you're starting to look forward to it."

"Not really," Stacy answered truthfully in a quiet and unemotional voice. "I've really enjoyed myself here."

There was a slight pause as if Cord was mulling over her reply. "I imagined you'd be glad to be going back where you belong."

Involuntarily Stacy stiffened at Cord's phrase. A flash of her old anger returned at his pompous attitude of always knowing what would be best for her. She quelled the urge to make a retort and continued gazing into the fire.

"Have you and Carter set a date for the wedding?" Cord asked, flicking a twig into the fire.

"No. That's something we'll probably do when we get back," Stacy replied, not letting the hurt seep into her words. Her pride said it was better to let him think that there was going to be a wedding.

"You'll send me an invitation?"

"Of course," she answered, straightening her legs and leaning back on her hands as she scowled into the fire. "Are you going to send me one to yours?"

"Mine?" Cord queried, straightening slowly at her words.

"I forgot I wasn't supposed to know," Stacy answered airily. "Though why you wanted to keep it from me, I don't know. It's pretty obvious the way Lydia's always over here that there's more than just the burning embers of an old flame."

"I see," an amused expression on Cord's face as he stared at the charred legs. "I suppose Lydia told you."

"More or less," she replied. She did all but write it on the wall, she thought to herself. "Now that you're released from your responsibility for me, you can go your merry way and I can go mine."

Seeing his dark head turn towards her in surprise she added, "I know about the letter from Carter's father too."

"Carter's father? And how do you know?"

"You left the letter in one of the desk drawers. I must say you went to great lengths to see to it that I kept under your watchful eye. It's too bad you didn't let me in on it. We might have got along better if I'd known what was going on."

"It didn't occur to me. You were a very headstrong girl. I only hope that Carter is successful in combating your more egocentric ideas." Cord seemed to be secretly amused, which greatly irritated Stacy.

"Carter understands me," she replied forcefully, lifting her chin defiantly.

"Oh, I'm sure he does," Cord laughed. "It's too bad he doesn't have more control over you."

"If he had, I never would have come here and all this would never have happened." Stacy's voice trailed off as a hint of melancholy crept into her voice.

"No, it wouldn't have," Cord agreed quietly, falling silent with her.

The crackling of twigs and rustling branches sounded the return of Hank and Carter.

"Ready to head back?" Carter asked her.

"Might as well," said Cord, rising and extending a hand to Stacy before Carter could intervene. "It's going to be a long day tomorrow."

THE RANCHYARD was packed with vehicles of every description from elegant El Dorados to broken-down ranch pick-ups. The auction itself had been over for two hours and the exodus of cars had just begun.

Stacy surveyed the long table that had been heaped with food earlier. So little was left of the vast quantities of meat, baked beans, potato salad, coleslaw, and breads that she sighed with relief that the appetites had been gauged so accurately. Already her group of ranch wives had started to clear the tables of leftover food.

"Are you through for the day?" Molly asked, a plump arm reaching out to fill the iced tea glasses.

"I've just been fired," Stacy laughed, "and ordered to join the fun."

"Good. It's mostly all neighbours left now," said Mary, hooking an arm in Stacy's and propelling her away from the table. "You're going to witness a good, old-fashioned party."

"Hey, where are you taking my hostess?" came the questioning laugh from behind them.

Halting abruptly, Stacy paled at the possessive tone in the voice. With a trembling heart, she felt the masculine hand rest on her shoulder.

"Cord!" Mary cried. "It's about time you got around to your guests. You've been with those horses all day."

"I see you've managed to extricate Stacy," he replied, smiling down at the silent form beside him. "You did a wonderful job, Stacy. I'm sorry I haven't had a chance to tell you earlier or to give you a hand which you didn't need."

"Thank you," Stacy stammered, a flush filling her cheeks at his unqualified praise. "But everyone has been good to me. I'm sure they covered a lot of my mistakes."

"You're too modest," Molly admonished. "With someone as sweet as you, people just naturally take you to their heart and do everything they can for you."

Tears pricked the back of Stacy's eyes at the woman's words. Knowing this to be her last day here, Stacy replied softly, "You've all made me feel as if this is my home and I'll never forget any of you for that."

Cord's hand tightened on her shoulder and the sudden pain forced Stacy to look into the tanned face. The questioning and confused look in his dark eyes rested on her face momentarily before turning to the other two women.

"This evening's party is doubling as a farewell party for Stacy. She's leaving us in the morning," Cord stated grimly.

In the midst of the barrage of protests and objections, Stacy experienced a pang of regret at the ambiguous statements she had made about her leaving, always saying "some time after the barbecue". If only they knew how little she really wanted to go!

"Why are you leaving so soon?" Mary asked. "I thought you'd be staying at least another week."

"Carter has to be back the first of the week, so we decided to go together," Stacy explained, ignoring the chill coursing through her as Cord removed his hand from her shoulder. "We can share the driving and the trip won't seem so long."

"The two of you are going alone?" Molly asked, frowning a little as she glanced at Cord.

"Tch, tch, Molly, you're showing your age," Cord mocked. "Remember this is the enlightened generation. Our moral codes are a little old-fashioned for them. Excuse me, I think it's time I mingled with some of the other guests."

Despite the light tone of Cord's voice as he had chided Molly, Stacy caught the underlying thread of bitterness in his words. Embarrassed by the implication, she faced the two women self-consciously, ignoring the retreating broad shoulders moving through the crowd.

"Have you decided to marry Carter?" Mary asked lightly as the sounds of guitars and fiddles drifted towards them.

"No," Stacy replied without thinking.

"Speak of the devil," Molly muttered as Stacy glanced around to see the sandy-haired Carter walking towards them. "So you're taking our favourite girl away from us tomorrow," Molly scolded.

"How else will I ever get her all to myself?" Carter asked, wrapping an arm around Stacy's shoulders. "Besides," he added, noting the hidden pain in Stacy's eyes, "a change of scenery might be advantageous."

Stacy missed the glance exchanged between mother and daughter as she looked up into Carter's questioning blue eyes.

"If you ladies don't mind, I think I'll dance with our hostess," smiled Carter, possessively moving Stacy in the direction of the strumming guitars.

At the edge of the dance floor, he turned her into his arms. He allowed a few steps to the tempo before speaking.

"What happened back there? I saw Cord leave before I arrived." His blue eyes studied the troubled look on her face. "What did he say to make you look like that?"

"It wasn't anything he said," Stacy murmured absently, catching sight of Cord watching them from the fringe of the crowd. "It's me, I guess," she sighed, forcing her eyes to Carter. "I just don't want to leave. I know it's the right thing to do."

"Stacy, are you even sure you're in love with him? If I thought I had a chance—" Urgency crowded out all caution as Carter gripped Stacy's shoulders. "Marry me, honey. I can make you happy, you know that."

"No, Carter." The chestnut head shook negatively, agitation and indecision in her voice.

"He's so much older than you. How do you know you're not using him to replace the father you lost?" Carter's voice grew desperate and demanding. "If I hadn't let you come out here, we'd have been married by now. Can't you see that, Stacy? You need an anchor. Let it be me. Say you'll marry me, Stacy, say it now before you regret it the rest of your life."

"No!" Stacy fairly shouted, trying to stem the whirlpool of persuasion Carter's words were drawing her into. "No," she repeated more emphatically, turning from his arms to face the happy dancing throng before them.

"Think about it, Stacy. How can you be sure?" Carter rushed.

"There you are, Stacy," came a masculine voice. "Don't you know it's not proper for the hostess to run off in the middle of the party?"

Through blurring eyes, Stacy recognized the stocky form of Bill Buchanan.

"Doctor!" a frantic trill to her words as he grasped her outstretched hand.

"You don't mind if I steal her for a dance, do you, Carter?" Bill asked, a merry twinkle in his eyes. "I'm too old to stand in line, and when the rest of the men get a good look at her that's just what I'd have to do."

The doctor whisked Stacy into the clearing where a lively tune was filling the air. As Stacy matched his bouncy steps, she momentarily glanced back to where Carter was standing. Her attention was caught by the tall figure standing steps away from him, separated only by the same trees in which she and Carter had sought seclusion moments ago. Forgetting her partner completely, Stacy stood motionless as terror raced through her at the realization that the turbulent fury flashing through Cord's eyes could only be caused by his overhearing her conversation with Carter. Suddenly Cord was moving through the dancers towards her. Hurriedly Stacy turned to her partner, ignoring his puzzled expression as she frantically hoped to lose herself among the other couples.

It was too late. The firm brown hand was gripping her shoulders as Cord expressed an abrupt apology to Dr. Buchanan and, without giving Stacy an opportunity to protest, forced her through the whirling couples. Away from the crowd, Stacy attempted futilely to pull away from Cord's hold.

"Let me go!" she cried desperately.

"Just shut up," Cord replied sharply. "You've done too much talking already."

"It's none of your business what happened between Carter and me." Stacy's temper flashed in her
brown eyes.

"I'll decide what's my business." The muscle in his
jaw twitched as Cord turned her towards the hacienda.

"What do you want from me?" Her voice trembled.

"Some straight answers for a start," said Cord
firmly, his voice threateningly low as a couple crossed
in front of them.

Walking on to the veranda, Cord muttered an im-
precation as he caught sight of guests gathered by the
pool. Without a hesitation in his stride, he turned her
towards the knoll above the house. Realizing they were
headed for the cemetery, Stacy glanced back at him
suspiciously.

"Why are we going up here?" she demanded,
slightly winded by the swift pace he was setting.

"It's probably the only place on this damn ranch
where there aren't any people," was the curt answer.

Reaching the top of the rise, he moved ahead,
dragging her behind him, until they were out of sight
of the people below. They stopped a few feet from the
iron fence. Releasing her arm, he took hold of a
breathless Stacy's shoulders.

"Why did you lie to me and let me believe you were
going to marry Carter?" he demanded.

"What does it matter?" Stacy moaned, trying to
wrench herself free of his hold.

"Do you want to go back? Do you want to leave here?" When she failed to answer, he shook her. "Answer me!"

"No!" she sobbed, fighting the answers he was seeking and the truth she couldn't bear him to know. "Please, Cord, don't!"

"Why don't you want to leave?"

"B-because—" she stammered. "Oh, Cord, please let me go."

"Stacy, I can't, not this time." His voice was suddenly tender and pleading. "Not until you tell me the truth. This time you've got to tell the truth."

Tears ran unchecked down her cheeks as she gazed into his tanned face with disbelief. Desperately she searched for assurance that the loving tone she had heard was not a mockery. He pulled her closer, as one side of his mouth lifted in encouragement. He whispered, "Don't look at me like that until you've answered me. Why don't you want to leave me?"

"Because—" she began, a flush filling her cheeks as a warm glow spread over her. "Because I love you. Cord, I—"

But his lips silenced the rest of her words. All resistance was gone as previously checked passions were unleashed in a burning embrace. When at last the fiery urgency was satisfied Cord's lips left Stacy's to travel to her eyes, cheeks, the curve of her neck as he whispered his endearments in the glory of love.

"Oh, Cord, Cord, I can't believe it," Stacy gasped, thrilling at his every touch. "You really love me?"

"I've loved you for an eternity." His deep voice choked with emotion like hers.

"You were so hateful to me," she accused, amidst another shower of kisses meant to silence her.

"I fell in love with you the day I found you lying unconscious on the plains. I knew then if anything happened to you my life wouldn't be worth living," Cord's voice was husky. "When you recovered and said you were leaving in a few weeks, I knew I had to find a way to make you stay, to make you love this land as I do."

"I do, Cord, I do," murmured Stacy.

"I know. I've never told you how proud I was of you and the way you took your place with the men on the drive and did your share of the work, except on occasions," he grinned.

"Were you jealous of Jim?" Stacy teased.

"I was jealous of anyone who touched you. Even your letters from Carter irritated me," he confessed.

"Look at the way you paraded Lydia around. She told me you were going to marry." Stacy's upturned face was earnest as she added, "That night on the veranda I thought you were pretending I was Lydia."

"How I wanted you that night, darling." His calloused hand traced the curve of her cheek. "When you recoiled from me—"

"Not from you, Cord. Never from you."

"Oh, the tangled webs we weave," Cord smiled.

"If you hadn't overheard my conversation with Carter and forced me to admit to you my love, would you have let me leave tomorrow?"

"I would have shown you no mercy, Miss Adams," Cord mocked gruffly.

"No quarter asked," Stacy replied with a smile, lifting her face for his kiss.

"And none given, Stacy," Cord murmured, inches away from her lips. "Now that you're finally mine, I'll never let you go. And there'll be no fancy wedding. We're going to be married as soon as we can. You understand that."

"Yes, Cord, yes," Stacy answered fervently, yielding once again to his embrace.

. . . and now an exciting preview of

AMERICAN PIE

**The first title in
Harlequin American Romance's
celebration of a
Century of American Romance.**

Join American Romance in a nostalgic look back at the 20th Century—at the lives and loves of American men and women from the turn of the century to the dawn of the year 2000.

Relive the moments...recapture the memories. The Century of American Romance series starts in June in Harlequin American Romance. In one of the four American Romance titles each month, for the next twelve months, we'll take you back to the decade of the 20th century, starting with AMERICAN PIE.

The year is 1896. Lucie Kolska, a Polish immigrant, enters the U.S. at Ellis Island. So does Jamie Kelly, an Irish immigrant. They came to America to find their slice of the pie and each has a promising future. What does America have to offer them? Can they find their dreams?

Look for AMERICAN PIE in June at your favorite retail outlet.

A CENTURY OF
1890's **AMERICAN** 1990's
ROMANCE

The women...the men...the passions...
the memories...

HARLEQUIN
American Romance®

MARGARET
ST. GEORGE

☆ 1890's ☆
A M E R I C A N
P I E

A CENTURY OF
1890's **AMERICAN** 1990's
ROMANCE

Chapter One

Seen from the water the main building on Ellis Island resembled a sprawling red-brick palace replete with soaring turrets and sun-tipped domes, a formidable island fortress guarding the portals to America. Those immigrants standing at the ship's railing swallowed hard and gripped the rail in mounting anxiety. What occurred on this small island and within that intimidating, authoritative-looking building would decide whose dreams came true and who would be denied entrance to the world's depository of hope.

Lucie Kolska, pale and trembling with nerves and trepidation, followed her cousin Petor up the wide sweep of the grand staircase and finally into a cavernous hall with a ceiling so high that two trapped birds darted and swooped beneath the arches. Hundreds of people milled about in confusion until a uniformed official herded them into the famed Ellis Island pens. Like cattle, they entered a tortuous maze defined by iron pipe rails that wound toward the front of the enormous hall.

Though the din in the room was thunderous, Lucie imagined she could hear the fearful pounding of her heart. From this day forward she would never hear mention of the Tower of Babel without remembering Ellis Island. Lucie could hear the sounds of fretful voices as people called and shouted questions in a dozen languages. Uniformed men yelled instructions. Hawkers from the booths near the door screamed enticements to visit the money-changing booth, the job-placement counter, the transportation center. If the noise wasn't enough to cause a headache, the odors were. The smell of nervous perspiration and closely bunched humanity overhung the packed lines like a sour miasma. As Lucie inched through the pens toward the medical examiner and the immigration authorities, she smelled urine, sweat, soiled clothing and occasionally the sharp fatty pungency of sausage.

One hour passed, then two, and still the line stretched in front of her, moving forward at a snail's pace. Heat mounted in the room and an elderly woman to Lucie's right fainted. And with each step forward, the level of anxiety increased. Lucie wet dry lips, then touched her glove to the numbered tag pinned to her coat. It would have been comforting to know what to expect. The medical examiner did not frighten her too badly; she knew she was strong and in good health. She didn't cough or limp as some did; her eyes were not red or crusted. She had no unusual growths, no skin eruptions.

But just thinking about the infamous twenty-nine questions raised a tremor of apprehension and caused

Lucie's lips and hands to shake. Everyone knew the twenty-nine questions must be answered correctly but no one knew what those questions were. Everyone was terrified they would fail and be turned back.

"Stop biting your lips, it makes you look suspicious," her cousin Petor advised from directly behind her. "They'll think you're an anarchist."

"Me?" The idea was absurd but her heart lurched. Here was one more thing to worry about. Instead of chewing her lower lip, she twisted her gloves around the rope handle of her reticule.

"Number four hundred and eight-two," a uniformed official called a moment later, screaming to be heard about the pandemonium roaring through the hall.

Lucie started violently, then stood paralyzed with fear and dread, her eyes as wide as daisies. She felt as if giant fingers squeezed her chest and she could not breathe, could not step beyond the iron pipe rails. Petor gave her a gentle push, though, breaking her paralysis, and she stumbled forward.

The official inspected the tag pinned to her coat, requested her name, then placed a check mark on his list. "In there," he said indifferently, jerking his head toward a door behind him.

Lucie swallowed hard, pressed both hands over her thudding heart, and glanced back at Petor hoping for a nod of encouragement. But her cousin's expression indicated he felt as worried as she about being returned to Poland. *Please, God,* she prayed silently before she drew a deep breath, squared her shoulders and timidly stepped into the medical examiner's room.

"Over here," someone called. Ordinarily Lucie considered herself a capable young woman, able to contend with life's exigencies, but these were not ordinary circumstances. So much depended upon the next moments.

The examination room was larger than she had expected, partitioned into cubicles created by cloth hung over lengths of rope. While the arrangement allowed adjustment for greater or lesser numbers of cubicles, the cubicles provided scant privacy as the fronts were open for all to see into. When her summons was repeated in French and German, Lucie started and hurried forward, murmuring apologies and averting her eyes from an anxious-looking man disrobing in the far corner. A large dark growth covered the upper portion of his chest.

"Doctor John Waithe with the United States Public Health Service." After introducing himself, a balding man beckoned her forward with an impatient gesture. He matched the number on her coat to the papers he held, then ordered her to walk back and forth along the wall, watching to see if she limped. "There is nothing to fear," he said in a voice that sounded tired. He studied her closely, then made a series of rapid checks down a form. "Sit down, please."

Dr Waithe's expressionless assurance did nothing to calm Lucie's racing heart, and her mouth was so dry she swallowed repeatedly. While he peered into her eyes, checking for trachoma, and examined her ears, throat and teeth, Lucie tried to see what was happening to the man with the growth on his chest. When the doctor instructed her to rise, she turned toward the cubicle opening and saw the man in the corner had dropped his head in his hands and was sitting in silence as his wife screamed and wrung her hands.

"You may go." Not looking up from his forms. Dr. Waithe waved toward a door she had failed to notice until now.

Clasping shaking hands against her quilted skirt, Lucie swallowed a lump the size of a biscuit. She could not speak above a whisper. "Are you turning me away?"

Now he glanced up and managed a weary smile. "No, Miss Kolska. You appear to be in excellent health."

Relief weakened her knees. Then she remembered the questions and a fresh onslaught of anxiety overwhelmed her. Inside the second room a half dozen officials directed questions at a half dozen trembling respondents. Lucie thanked heaven a stool had been provided. Her shaking legs could not have held her upright throughout the ordeal.

A man with a thick dark mustache pointed to a stool before him. "Do you speak English?"

"Yes, sir," she whispered, averting her eyes from his uniform. Petor had insisted no one in America feared uniforms, but old habits were hard to break. At home a man in uniform could conscript a brother or father into the army, could seize a wife or daughter for an hour's pleasure, could take the winter's food from the cellar. And one could do nothing but smile and bow and push the hatred deep inside.

"Can you read and write?"

"Slowly, but...yes, I can." The official murmured a word of approval and placed a check mark on his papers. Feeling bewildered, Lucie's dark eyes widened. Was it possible she had already answered two of the dreaded questions? Surely not.

"What kind of work do you do?"

"Farm work. Women's work."

He wrote on his papers. "Where are you going?"

"Here. To America." She bit her lip in fright when he frowned and it appeared she had answered incorrectly. "I'm going to live in New York City of America."

He nodded. "Is someone meeting you?"

She didn't understand. The questions were so simple there had to be a trick she was too nervous to comprehend.

"Are you a polygamist?" When Lucie didn't respond, the official glanced at her over the top of his papers. "Do you believe in having two husbands or two wives?"

Her mouth dropped, then she laughed aloud, something she had not dreamed she would do during the questioning. "No!"

"Do you plan to overthrow the government of the United States of America now or in the future?"

Did anyone ever answer yes? Suddenly she understood the questions were not a trap for the unwary, not devised to turn people away. Her shoulders sagged with relief, and confidence flickered in her gaze. She identified the same expressions on the faces around her, suspicion, disbelief, then dawning elation.

Finally, it was over and the official smiled. "Welcome to America, miss. You may remove your tag now. Here is your landing card." She accepted the card with dazed pride and carefully slipped it inside her shirtwaist for safekeeping. "Collect your baggage outside, then take the number three ferry to the city."

"I'm an American!" she whispered, hardly daring to believe. Tears of elation brimmed in her eyes. Because Petor had told her people shook hands in America, she thrust out her hand, caught the official's glove and pumped his arm up and down until he smiled and protested. "Thank you," she murmured enthusiastically. Shaking his hand wasn't enough, she wanted to shout and run and dance and jump in the air. "Oh, thank you, thank you!"

Outside the main building she stopped abruptly and breathed deeply of the bright June air, joyfully filling her lungs with an American breeze. Overhead the sky was clear and bottomless, as dazzlingly blue as the harbor waters rippling between Ellis Island and the towering city of New York. This was her home now, she thought, stunned by the idea of it. She had succeeded; she was an American.

Throwing out her arms and laughing aloud, Lucie spun in a circle that sent her skirts billowing and turned her toward the city skyline. Amazingly, some of the buildings appeared to be ten or even eleven stories tall. They scraped the very sky. The vision was so stupefying that she shifted her gaze, seeking a moment of perspective in the ordinary sight of gulls swooping above the docks. Dizzy with happiness, she wrapped her arms around her short dark jacket and hugged herself, feeling the landing card safe and real against her heart.

When she could bear another burst of excitement, she rose on tiptoe to see above the throngs of people jamming the grand staircase, shouting in excitement or confusion. Yes, there it was. Lucie could glimpse the crown and torch of Lady Liberty above the turrets and domes of the main building. Moisture dampened her eyes and her heart swelled with pride. Life was going to be wonderful here.

"I've found our baggage," Petor said, appearing at her side. After dropping their knotted bundles at her feet, he wiped the sweat from his forehead and smiled. "We're Americans now, ja?"

All trace of timidity and nervousness had vanished from Lucie's expression. Her dark eyes glowed with excitement. "I can't wait to see Stefan! Have you found him? And your brother?" Rising again on tiptoe, she tried to peer above the mass of people pushing and shoving around her. Although Petor stood beside her, she had to shout in his ear to be heard. An elbow knocked against her shoulder, a swinging bundle struck her hip and she clasped Petor's arm to steady herself. "Oh, dear. We'll never find Stefan in this crush!"

"I'll search for them," Petor shouted near her hat brim. "You stay with our baggage." Leaning forward, he tapped the shoulder of a man who was trying not to be pushed into the bundles at Lucie's feet. "Sir, could I impose upon you to protect my cousin while I search for our party?"

The stranger turned and his warm dark eyes settled on Lucie in a look of unabashed admiration. "I would be honored to serve your cousin, sir."

Lucie gazed into those eyes, the color of freshly turned earth, and a tiny shiver ran through her body as if lightning had struck nearby. Something tightened inside and suddenly she couldn't breathe properly. Her lips parted and her eyes widened. The handsome young man standing before her exuded a sense of confidence she had not observed today, his self-assurance stood out like an island of calm amidst the chaos surging around them.

Aware that her steady gaze was immodest, Lucie tried to look away from him, but she couldn't. She watched him remove a tweed cap to reveal a thatch of auburn hair that glowed as warmly in the sunlight as did his smile. When Lucie realized he was staring at her as intently as she stared at him, a rush of confusion heated her cheeks and she hastily ducked her head, concealing her blush beneath the brim of her straw hat.

At home in Wlad if a man stared at a woman the way this man stared at her, as if he were enchanted, the villagers said he had been struck by love's elbow. The blush deepened on Lucie's cheeks and her heart skipped a beat. No man had ever looked at her this directly, as if he were seeing something hidden from the rest of the world. The experience was thrilling and confusing, a strange, wonderful way to begin her new life in America.

"It isn't true, you know," her protector said after Petor had plunged into the shouting crowd rushing and pushing past them. Bending slightly, he peered beneath her hat brim to examine her face. "American streets are paved with mud and horse droppings just like anywhere else."

"I know," Lucie murmured, startled that he had read her mind and also feeling a twinge of disappointment. She hadn't believed the streets of America were paved with gold, not really, or that shopkeepers dined on silver platters. But it had been exciting to imagine.

She dared another look and bit her lower lip. As he was still bending near her, she inhaled the sunshiny scent of his tweed jacket and the pleasing male scents of hair oil and a faint underlying hint of clean, honest perspiration. Unsettled by her response to his attention, by the peculiar turmoil his nearness caused, Lucie pressed her hands together and ducked her head again. Never before could she recall being this intensely aware of a man. She felt as if five hundred people had faded away leaving only the two of them standing at the base of the grand staircase.

"As there's no one to introduce us...I'm Jamie Kelly, recently of Dublin, Ireland."

"Were you aboard the *Poutansia*?" Lucie inquired, peeking up at him. She did not recall any Irish on board. Certainly she had seen no man as handsome as this one.

Jamie Kelly turned the full force of his gaze on her and for an instant Lucie could not breathe. Above his waistcoat, his collar and shirtfront looked freshly starched, and his dark trousers and coat were a higher quality than any she had observed during the voyage. Moreover, he was clean shaven whereas the fashion of the day decreed mustaches and beards. His smooth jaw indicated a man who was unafraid to proclaim his individuality, a man who danced to his own music.

"I arrived last week. Oh, I see. Why am I here today?" His gaze lifted to the wide curving staircase behind her. "I hoped to find a position at the labor exchange."

The buzz and roar of people shouting just inches away made it difficult to hear. Some of the accents were familiar to Lucie, many were not. She decided none sounded as soft and melodious as Jamie Kelly's deep rolled *R*s.

His steady gaze compelled her to speak, and indeed there was much to learn, although she didn't dare raise the questions she longed to ask, questions regarding him.

"I won't bite," Jamie Kelly gently assured her, smiling as if he had again guessed her thoughts. "So, what do you think of America? Is it what you expected?" Although he had to shout, he spoke without looking away from her face.

"I—I'm so relieved about the questions. I was terribly worried about them." Because his unwavering admiration made her cheeks feel hot, Lucie dropped her gaze to the cap he turned in his hands. Surely it wasn't proper to stand this close and stare into each other's eyes. She didn't know what had come over her. Stepping back, she pretended to examine the city waiting across the sail-dotted harbor. "It's so big, isn't it? And so noisy. Do you image America would be so big?"

He grinned at seeing the excitement shining in her dark eyes. "And filled with marvels."

She could not wait to see those marvels. "Oh, please tell me about them."

Sunlight glowed like fire on his auburn hair as he tilted his head to smile down at her. "I wouldn't dream of spoiling your pleasure, though I'm tempted. You must see for yourself." Then he seemed to realize he was making her uncomfortable and he cleared his throat and shifted to scan the crowd spilling around them. "Is someone meeting you?"

"My brother, Stefan," she said, her face lighting. "I haven't seen him in two years. He's the one who paid for my passage," she confided with pride. "Our Stefan has a home of his own and a steady job. After only two years, can you imagine? In America anything is possible," she added, thinking how long it would take to acquire a home in Wlad.

When Jamie Kelly laughed, the rich rolling sound surrounded her with warmth and made Lucie smile in return. Suddenly she wondered if he thought her wool gloves and quilted skirt were too heavy for spring, wondered if he could tell she wore three blouses, two skirts and all of her petticoats. Then she realized Jamie Kelly's tweed coat and worsted trousers must be as uncomfortably warm as her quilted skirt and winter jacket.

"I'm sure you'll find work soon," Lucie assured him, overflowing with the confidence of being in America and her own natural optimism.

A frown drew Jamie Kelly's thick eyebrows together as he studied the masses of people thrusting toward the ferries. "The economy is depressed right now and more people arrive every day. Jobs aren't easy to find."

"Perhaps you aren't seeking in the right places, Mr. Kelly." Another deep blush bloomed on Lucie's cheeks. What must he think of her, who was but hours off the ship, that she would dare to offer advice? An apology hovered on her lips. It was suddenly important to her that he think well of her.

He said something but she didn't hear as Petor reappeared, shouting and tugging at her arm. "I've found them. They're waiting for us by the ferry." A thrill of excitement lifted Lucie's expression as she realized she would be seeing Stefan within minutes. Petor raised his hat to Jamie Kelly, then swung their bundles up on his shoulders.

"Wait!"

But the noise was too overwhelming, and Lucie couldn't hear what Mr. Kelly shouted as Petor impatiently nudged her forward into the crowd. There was time for one quick glance over her shoulder, time to feel the violent blush that heated her cheeks, then the throng closed over the handsome Irishman and he vanished in the crush. For an instant Lucie experienced a startling sense of loss, as if something magical had been stolen from her.

There was no time to examine her reaction as she spotted Stefan standing beside the rails in front of the ferry, leaning forward, scanning the sea of people. Joy filled her and she forgot everything except seeing her brother again. "Over here!" she shouted, rising on tiptoe to wave, all the while knowing he couldn't hear.

Fixing her gaze on his dear face, Lucie pushed forward, dodging elbows and bundles. Stefan sported a new hat and a sturdy coat she noticed proudly, but surprisingly he still wore the same heavy trousers she had mended half a dozen times before he sailed to America.

"Stefan!" Laughing and crying Lucie flung herself into his bearlike embrace. Stefan lifted her high, then hugged her tightly to his chest.

"Let me look at you," he said finally, blinking away moisture as he held her away to see her better.

"No, no, speak English," Lucie insisted, straightening her hat and wiping tears of happiness from her eyes. "We must speak English. We're American now!"

Holding hands they studied each other, searching for changes. After a moment Lucie happily decided Stefan was still the brother she knew. Two years older and a bit thinner perhaps, definitely in need of a haircut and a trim for his mustache, but he was still her

Stefan. His brown eyes were as determined as she remembered, his jaw as stubborn as ever it had been.

Looking at him was like observing a blend of their parents. Stefan had inherited their father's imposing powerful physique, but like Lucie, his face and hands bore the more delicate mark of their mother. No one spoke of it, but everyone in Wlad knew Count Bartok had sired Marta Kolska. Lucie and Stefan had inherited their illustrious grandfather's thin nose, well-shaped mouth and aristocratic profile.

"You've grown up, Luticia," Stefan said softly. "How old are you now, eighteen? Nineteen? And such a beauty. I'll have to guard you from dozens of suitors."

Lucie laughed but she thought of the attractive Irishman and love's elbow and the color in her cheeks deepened to a becoming shade of rose. "I'm almost nineteen, still three years younger than you. What else have you forgotten?" she asked, teasing him. Then the ferry's whistle blasted above and Lucie covered her ears as Stefan accepted her bundle from Petor and guided her up the plank and onto the boat.

They were jammed too tightly aboard the ferry to talk and crowded too near the center to see much of anything. Thankfully the harbor trip was brief and within minutes a sea of people flowed down the plank and onto the wharves.

Lucie's first impression of America, once she put Jamie Kelly firmly out of her mind, was the fishy scent of oysters. Before being jostled forward, she paused to gaze at the piles of oyster shells littering the dock area, higher than a man and stretching along the waterside as far as she could see. Everywhere she looked she saw signs advertising oyster saloons or oyster bars. She wondered if Americans ate anything else. Then her attention was captured by the horse-drawn wagons racing along the street, spilling lumps of coal and, incredibly, bits of ice.

Her eyes rounded in amazement. "Ice?" she asked Stefan, who grinned at her. "In June?" Truly America was a wondrous place.

She could hardly wrench her attention from the thick traffic long enough to murmur goodbye to Petor and his brother. "Thank you for escorting me," she whispered, distracted. She shook Petor's hand and wished him well. "If Minnesota is not too far away, you must come for Sunday supper."

"Thank you," Petor agreed solemnly, gazing wide-eyed at the rush and din of the street traffic. "We will."

Laughing, Stefan swung her bundle over his shoulder and led her past the enormous mounds of oyster shells. "Minnesota is very far away," he said, but Lucie wasn't listening.

She watched the blur of galloping traffic with large astonished eyes. There were drays and beer wagons, tall swaying furniture vans and wagon beds filled with shad and mackerel. There were also vegetable wagons and butcher carts, chandler's van and flower carts, and here and there a carriage fit for a prince. Even along the wharves the facing buildings rose five and six stories tall and here as everywhere within the city, painted advertisements sprouted over the building walls like brilliantly colored vines.

Later, Lucie couldn't recall how she and Stefan managed to cross the street, dodging spinning wheels and galloping hooves, but when next she remembered to catch her breath, Stefan was paying a horse car conductor two pennies and they were entering a stiflingly hot box, packed as tightly as the ferry. A man spit a stream of tobacco juice into the straw covering the floor then rose and offered Lucie his seat. She hesitated, not certain if she should accept until Stefan nodded.

The scene glimpsed through the dusty window caused her heart to pound with excitement and apprehension. For the most part she could not see much beyond the four lanes of traffic that sped past them so breathtakingly close that her heart lurched in fear of collision. But occasionally she caught sight of the buildings, hundreds and hundreds of buildings, pressed tightly one against the other, block after unbroken block of glass and stone and iron work. And more people than she had ever dared to imagine could inhabit a single place.

Standing above her, swaying with the motion of the ceiling strap, Stefan announced the streets as they passed, lower Broadway, then Canal Street, but the names meant nothing to her. The crush of traffic and people and noise overwhelmed Lucie's senses. She hadn't expected the city to be so busy, so large, so exciting. And nothing had prepared her for the sheer numbers.

Wistfully she recalled the handsome Irishman with the dancing eyes whom she had naively supposed she would meet again. Now she comprehended a second encounter would be akin to a miracle. Love's elbow might have struck them but they were lost to each other. Before she could experience the full weight of regret, she heard Stefan shout to the conductor and beckon her forward. Eagerly, Lucie gathered her skirts and flew down the steps to the street, her spirits lifting in fresh excitement.

She could not have described what she expected to see because she had not known what to expect. But surely this could not be where Stefan lived. Her exuberance faded to dismay as she peered into the narrow filthy street opening in front of her.

The paving stones ended where Elizabeth Street began. A haze of manure-scented dust overhung the street, which seemed even narrower due to the line of broken sagging wagons abandoned along the crumbling curb. Beneath the wagons and between them lay piles of garbage rotting in the afternoon heat, swarming with a dark covering of flies.

Pressing an uncertain hand to her breast, Lucie examined the four- and five-story wooden tenements that blocked any sunlight from the street. Between lines of grayish laundry crisscrossing overhead, she glimpsed broken window panes and listless children sitting on sagging metal fire escapes that looked as if they might pull loose at any moment and crash into the street below. The people hurrying past looked exhausted and anxious, some wore disturbing expressions of bewilderment or defeat. The clothing she noticed was unlike the fashionable ensembles she had admired on Broadway. Here the attire was mended and hastily assembled, in need of a good wash and a brushing. The lowered heads and bent backs were as shockingly familiar as the despair and hopelessness she had left behind in Wlad.

"Stefan?" she whispered, swallowing with difficulty.

"This way," he said gruffly, his gaze not meeting hers.

They stepped off the paving stones into the dust and powdered manure overhanging Elizabeth Street, and immediately Lucie realized the same closely packed buildings that blocked the sunlight also trapped the heat. Before they had walked more than a few steps, a trickle of perspiration rolled down her throat, and patches of dampness spread under her arms.

The heat and the stench of raw garbage, horse manure, outhouses and too many unwashed bodies packed into too little space made her feel dizzy. Pausing, she clasped Stefan's arm, recoiling from the sympathy she read in passing glances that swept over her bundle then herself before they turned away.

"Through here," Stefan said, striding toward a dark narrow passageway leading between two buildings.

"Stefan?" she asked again, staring up at him. But Stefan stood silently, her bundle over his broad shoulder, frowning at a beer wagon that lumbered along the street, stirring dust and flies and the odors of hardship and desperation.

She caught her lower lip between her teeth, then lifted her skirts above her boots and drew a breath before she hastened through the dark tunnel that Stefan indicated. At the end of the opening lay a small shaded courtyard of sorts, hemmed by tall buildings that trapped the stench from a row of tin-roofed latrines. Lucie halted and pressed a handkerchief to her nose, her eyes watering above the edge.

The persistent drip from a rusted pump in the center of the courtyard had created a dark puddle of slowly spreading mud. Broken cobbles littered the ground, along with heaps of refuse as fly blown and malodorous as the piles in the street. A half dozen children played in the gray dirt, three women labored over laundry tubs near the row of outhouses. A tan dog sniffed at a mound of ashes and cinders. There was not a scrap of green in the stifling courtyard, only a few yellowed lines of weeds dying in the heat.

For an instant Stefan met her gaze, then he moved past her, toward a door hanging from its hinges. Inside, a dark littered stairway stinking of urine and cooking odors led up to a hallway cast in permanent night. When Stefan opened one of the doors, Lucie stumbled inside and crossed directly to the window, leaning to inhale a long breath of hot stale air through the broken pane.

Although she was high above the street, on the third floor, higher than she had been before, the din of wheels and harness and an erupting street brawl sounded as if she were standing in their midst. Numbed by what she had seen, she straightened slowly and turned to inspect Stefan's home, now hers.

The smallness impressed her first, the sense of not having enough space to breathe. There was nothing in the bare-floored room but a scarred table, a mismatched set of chairs and a cast-iron stove, cranky from the look of it. Slowly Lucie unpinned her hat and removed her jacket, then hung them on the exposed nails driven into the wall near the door.

Darkness formed her second impression. One of the walls might have been light colored once, now it was dark with smoke and age. Brown wallpaper bubbled and peeled from the other walls, shadowed deeper in spots by oily stains.

A cramp of homesickness tightened Lucie's small shoulders. With all her heart she longed to run home to her parents' snug bright cottage and the sweet green scent of the fields. In a week her mother would clip rosemary and thyme to spread over the new straw in the loft. The cottage would smell of spring and fresh herbs and her mother's lamb stew.

Knowing Stefan watched, not wanting him to recognize her shock and homesickness, Lucie smoothed shaking hands over her quilted skirt and walked to the stove blinking rapidly as she bent to inspect the rust-crusted oven door. When she could control the moisture welling in her eyes, she straightened and focused on a tin coffeepot that had boiled over and splattered the surface of the range.

"Exactly what I was wanting," she lied, thinking of the ice wagon she had seen and the children running behind to catch the chunks that had been jostled into the street. An hour ago she had not known it was possible to have ice in June. Now she longed for a tiny piece to press over her throat and face. "A good cup of hot coffee. Do we have cups? Yes, here they are." On the wooden shelf in front of her nose.

"There's another room," Stefan said stiffly, watching her. "Many have only one room."

"Then we are fortunate," Lucie said brightly. She followed him into a second minuscule room and waited while he struck a lucifer to light the windowless blackness. Two thin mattresses were rolled and tied and pushed against the wall. When they were opened for the night, there would not be space for anything else.

"I made a private place for you." Stefan pointed to a length of faded cloth strung across one corner.

"Thank you," Lucie whispered, swallowing the lump in her throat. She pressed his hand.

They returned to the kitchen and Lucie poured coffee, noticing the grounds were not fresh and the coffee was pale as tea. She sat across the table from Stefan and lowered her eyes from his painful expression.

"I'm sorry." He ran a hand through his hair and tugged his mustache, a gesture she remembered. "It isn't what you expected."

"We all thought—" Pressing her lips together, Lucie bit off what she had been about to say. His pride suffered enough, she could see it in his dark eyes, in the wooden set of his shoulders.

"After two years I had hoped to be able to rent something better." Frowning, Stefan looked into the cup he turned between his hands. "But even a small house rents for eight hundred to a thousand dollars a year. When a man earns a dollar a day..."

"What does our home rent for?" Lucie asked, looking at the peeling walls, the broken window pane.

"Three dollars a week."

Barter was the basis of the economy in Wlad. Lucie knew to the feather how many chickens were required to buy enough cloth for skirts for her mother and herself. A half dozen eggs equaled a loaf of good black bread. A pound of autumn honey equaled a bushel of winter apples. American coins confused her.

Using her fingers she counted and figured, then raised a look of concern. "After paying the rent, you have three dollars to live on. Is everything else in America so cheap that three dollars is enough?"

Stefan's laugh was harsh. "Nothing in America is cheap."

"But you saved my passage money—"

"Until this morning I rented space to two additional men."

"I see." She could not imagine three people sharing the space around her. But it required little imagination to recognize the hardship Stefan had endured to save the twenty-seven dollars required for her passage to America. "I will make this up to you," she said softly.

He waved the promise aside then leaned forward eagerly. "Lucie, tell me about home. Are the mother and father well? Is the barley out of the ground? Did Ivan Bobich clear his forest land? And my cow—has my cow calved yet?"

After pouring more coffee, Lucie assured him their parents were well, then she spoke of the village and village gossip until darkness gathered outside the window.

"I have news, too," Stefan announced when she finished speaking. A flush of color seemed to rise from his collar and his voice softened to a tone Lucie had not heard before. "I am to be married. As soon as there is money enough."

Surprise rounded Lucie's mouth, then she clapped her hands in delight and rushed to embrace him. "Oh, Stefan! What wonderful news. Tell me everything about her!"

"Her name is Greta Laskowski," Stefan said, smiling broadly. "Her people are from a village outside Warsaw. The family immigrated to America four years ago, but things did not go well for them. The parents died. Two sisters married and returned to Poland. Her brother went west." It seemed as if a cloud passed and Stefan's expression darkened. "Greta wanted to be here to welcome you, but her health has suffered lately. Already she thinks of you as a sister."

Moisture dampened Lucie's lashes. It would be good to have a sister in this strange confusing land. Reaching across the scarred table, she clasped Stefan's hand. "It is my turn to help you. I'll find work,

and in no time at all we'll save your marriage money."
She owed him that much.

The softness faded from Stefan's dark eyes. "I wish
it were that easy, Lucie," he said, shaking his head.
"Work is hard to find; the pay is low. Every day
hundreds of immigrants pour into the city, all desperate for work. Any man who demands decent wages
will find someone standing behind him willing to do
the same job for pennies." Frowning, he looked at the
darkness pressing against the window. "It's not like we
thought. Yes, there is opportunity here, but a man
must look hard to find it. It isn't enough to have two
hands and a strong back."

Determination firmed the lines of Lucie's mouth.
"I'll find something," she said brusquely. "Tomorrow we begin saving for your marriage to my new sister."

After Stefan lit the table lamp he examined her
expression, then laughed. "You sound like Greta.
Both of you can find a glimmer of sunlight in the
darkest shadow." He pressed Lucie's hand. "Tomorrow you must rest from your journey, then take a day
or so to explore. There's so much to see."

"Right now I need to explore for our supper." she
said, pushing up from the table. There was no meat in
the salt box beside the scuttle, but considering the heat
she hadn't really expected there would be. Nor was
there much of anything else.

In the end Lucie relied on her mother's recipe for
hard times and crumbled a hardening loaf of dark
bread into two cracked bowls she found on the shelf.

Though it added to the heat trapped in the room, she fed the stove until a pot bubbled then she poured the boiling water over the bread. After waiting a moment she poured off the excess water, added a generous amount of salt and pepper then stirred in a spoonful of the cooking grease she found in a crock on the back of the stove.

"Even when I'm rich," Stefan said with a wink, "I'll want Greta to prepare water-bread to remind me of home."

Lucie laughed and refrained from mentioning that no one in Wlad imagined people in America ate water-bread.

But she thought of it later when she was lying on her thin mattress in the tar-black second room, listening to an argument on the other side of the wall that sounded as if it were taking place at her elbow. She listened to the angry despairing voices, listened to the scrabble of mice—she hoped it was only mice—running up the walls, listened to Stefan's soft snore. A tear spilled from her eyes and dropped to the mattress.

She had not expected that she and Stefan would live in luxury or splendor. But neither had she expected squalor. As poor as they were, the villages in Wlad had fresh clean air and plentiful sunshine. And flowers on the sills. No one lived above an outhouse or piled garbage in his yard.

It was also true there was no hope for change in Wlad, no opportunity for a young man or woman to better themselves. Inheritance had carved the land into smaller and smaller plots and each year the soil seemed less fertile than the year before, the harvest less plentiful. People went to bed hungry in Wlad and shivered before empty grates when the snows came. And always there was the fear of the soldiers who might swoop through the village burning and pillaging for an evening's amusement.

Life would be better in America. But Lucie stared into the darkness and remembered the faces in Elizabeth Street. She knew those faces. Faces frozen by anxiety, faces holding fear inside. Hungry faces, ill faces, faces reflecting the uncertainty of tomorrow. Had they arrived in the land of plenty as filled with hope and excitement as she? What had happened between Ellis Island and Elizabeth Street?

Was America no more than a golden myth? No, she thought with a shudder of rejection. No soldiers would come in the night. No tax collector would appear in the morning. Her belly was full and she had two rooms to call her own. Stefan had work and so would she. They were young and strong and willing to wait for the opportunity that would surely come, as it never would in Wlad.

Lying in the darkness, listening to the sounds of Stefan's snores and the noise within and beyond the walls, Lucie finally let herself remember the Irishman whose dark eyes had made her shiver in the sunlight. Where was he tonight? Would she ever see him again? It didn't seem possible that fate had brought them together only to cast them apart.

She recalled the exhilaration she had felt when she met Jamie Kelly, followed by the shock and disap-

pointment of seeing where she and Stefan would live.
Her first day in America had been strange and bewildering—and not at all what she had expected.

IN THE MORNING she fried the last of the bread for
Stefan's breakfast and sent him downstairs to empty
the slop bucket and join the line waiting to pump fresh
water for coffee and washing.

Shortly after Stefan departed for work, a sliver of
sunlight slipped across the window's broken pane and
Lucie stared at the light, mesmerized, suspecting it
would be the last sunshiny brightness she would see
today.

Before Stefan returned, bringing bread, cheese and
sausage for their supper, she had replaced the linen on
the mattresses with the sheets she brought from home,
had scrubbed the rooms from floor to ceilings, had
polished the lamp chimneys and had restored a semblance of respectability to the stove.

The next day, marshaling her courage, she donned
her hat and gloves and timidly ventured outside determined to explore her new world. The bewildering
array of streets and cross streets and back alleyways
overwhelmed her but she made herself swallow the
fear that lodged in her throat. The trick was to proceed slowly, memorizing her steps, progressing a bit
farther each day.

By the end of the week she discovered the Hester
Street market and learned the best buys could be made
late in the day when the stall owners and pushcart
vendors prepared to close shop for the evening. She

found the station for the elevated, though she didn't dare venture inside, and made herself stand and watch and listen to the hideous shriek of hot metal until she no longer felt like running from the noise and belching cinders. She located the corners where the red horse cars stopped and examined the wares offered by the pushcarts in every street—secondhand clothing, secondhand food and scissors, eyeglasses and scraps of wood and old nails. Eventually she walked to Broadway and stood enchanted before huge glass panes that displayed items of such unimaginable luxury they took her breath away.

She discovered streets that had formed into small countries, Italians here, strange exotic Orientals there, Hebrews and Slavs and Greeks, each group claiming a section of the city for themselves. She found the dumps where the ragpickers worked and the wharves and factories that fouled the air with soot and the sulfur smell of blast furnaces.

And always she watched for Mr. Kelly, hoping to turn the next corner and encounter him. When she did not, her disappointment was acute. As Lucie prided herself on possessing a practical nature not given to flights of fancy, her constant hope of meeting Mr. Kelly troubled her. She did not understand why she could not forget him. Or why she did not wish to.

Aware she acted foolishly and out of character, she nevertheless scanned the streets and walkway traffic, seeking a bright auburn head, a broad set of shoulders, teeth as white as bleached bone. Once she heard a man laugh and she stopped, feeling her cheeks heat with anticipation. But when she turned, it was not him and her shoulders dropped with disappointment.

She found no work, either. "Tomorrow I'll try the factories," she assured Stefan at the end of her second week in America. She considered their supper of cold potato pie and yesterday's bread and figured the cost in her mind.

"The factories have been sacking people," Stefan informed her. "Greta worries whether she'll have a job tomorrow."

Lucie still hadn't met Greta, which was a continuing disappointment, but already she admired the young woman's courage. Though ill, Greta rose each day and went to work. "Is she feeling any better?"

Stefan carried their supper plates to the tub of hot water on top of the stove. A worried frown drew his brow. "A little. She's so eager to meet you, worried what you must think that she hasn't greeted you. I hope by next week..."

Lucie finished her glass of warm beer and mopped her neck. It was as hot tonight as it had been last night. Heat engulfed the city, squeezing the air from every breath, turning the streets into dry choking powder. The newspapers compared this summer to the heat wave of 1896, three years ago, and the numbers of people and animals who had died of heat-related illness.

It worried her that Stefan carried his mattress up to the tenement rooftop to sleep, hoping for a breath of cooler air. At least once a week the newspapers reported the death of someone who had fallen from a rooftop.

Lucie sighed. It was imperative that she find work soon. Stefan had shown her the hiding place under the loose board in the second room where he kept his money. The small cache was steadily dwindling. Standing, thinking about it, she smoothed her hands over her apron then washed the supper dishes, saving the water for the morning.

"Tomorrow I'll bring your noonday meal to the work site," she said before Stefan departed to carry his mattress up to the roof. When he protested she turned to face him. "Please, Stefan. I need to feel useful. It will give me something to do until I find work."

After he left, she sat in the hot thick darkness wearing only her petticoat and shift, holding their remaining coins in her hand. Slowly, she counted them again, hoping she had erred.

Long after the night rustlings died in the street, Lucie continued to sit in the darkness beside the window, looking at the sagging shutters on the tenement facing her. Right now her goal of earning Stefan's marriage money seemed as far away as the handsome Irishman who continued to haunt her dreams.

A bittersweet ache settled in Lucie's small bosom. She wondered if Jamie Kelly had found a job, wondered if he remembered their brief meeting at Ellis Island, wondered if he thought about her as frequently as she found herself thinking about him.

HARLEQUIN *Temptation*

This May, look for

Having Faith
BARBARA DELINSKY

*Faith Barry knew making love with Sawyer Bell
had been a big mistake. He was an old, dear friend,
and they were representing opposing clients in a
complicated divorce case. She wished they'd never
crossed that line between lovers and friends. But they
had. Now Faith faced a new dilemma—how to keep
the courtroom battle out of the bedroom....*

HAVING FAITH, Barbara Delinsky's nine-
teenth Temptation, is as fresh and exciting as
her first, an accomplishment that has earned
Barbara yet another Award of Excellence,
Harlequin's official recognition of its finest
authors. And Barbara *is* one of the finest.

Don't miss HAVING FAITH (Temptation #297)
in May, only from Harlequin Temptation.

This April, don't miss Harlequin's new Award of
Excellence title from

Harlequin Presents...

CAROLE MORTIMER

Award of Excellence

elusive as the unicorn

When Eve Eden discovered that Adam
Gardener, successful art entrepreneur, was
searching for the legendary English artist, The
Unicorn, she nervously shied away. The Unicorn's
true identity hit too close to home....

Besides, Eve was rattled by Adam's
mesmerizing presence, especially in the light
of the ridiculous coincidence of their names—
and his determination to take advantage of it!
But Eve was already engaged to marry her
longtime friend, Paul.

Yet Eve found herself troubled by the different
choices Adam and Paul presented. If only the
answer to her dilemma didn't keep eluding her...

HP1258-1